THIS BOOK
BELONGS TO

By the Same Author

Emily Eyefinger

Emily Eyefinger, Secret Agent

Emily Eyefinger and the Lost Treasure

Emily Eyefinger and the Black Volcano

Emily Eyefinger's Alien Adventure

Emily Eyefinger and the Devil Bones

Emily Eyefinger and the Balloon Bandits

Emily Eyefinger and the Ghost Ship

Piggott Place

Piggotts in Peril

Selby's Secret

Selby Speaks

Selby Screams

Selby Supersnoop

Selby Spacedog

Selby Snowbound

Selby Surfs

Selby Snaps!

Selby's Joke Book

Selby Splits

Selby's Selection

Selby's Stardom

Selby's Side-splitting Joke Book

Selby Sorcerer

Selby Scrambled

SELBY'S SECRET

DUNCAN BALL

with illustrations by Allan Stomann

Angus&Robertson
An imprint of HarperCollins*Publishers*

Angus&Robertson
An imprint of HarperCollins*Publishers*, Australia

First published in Australia in 1985
This edition published in 2004
by HarperCollins*Publishers* Pty Limited
ABN 36 009 913 517
A member of the HarperCollins*Publishers* (Australia) Pty Limited Group
www.harpercollins.com.au

Text copyright © Duncan Ball 1985
Illustrations copyright © Allan Stomann 1985

HarperCollinsPublishers
25 Ryde Road, Pymble, Sydney, NSW 2073, Australia
31 View Road, Glenfield, Auckland 10, New Zealand
77–85 Fulham Palace Road, London W6 8JB, United Kingdom
2 Bloor Street East, 20th floor, Toronto, Ontario M4W 1A8, Canada
10 East 53rd Street, New York NY 10022, USA

National Library of Australia Cataloguing-in-Publication data:

Ball, Duncan, 1941– .
    Selby's secret.
    ISBN 0 207 20004 1.
    1. Dogs – Juvenile fiction. I. Stomann, Allan. II. Title.
A823.3

Cover design and internal design by Christa Edmonds
Typeset in 14/18pt Bembo by HarperCollins Design Studio
Printed and bound in Australia by Griffin Press on 60gsm Bulky Paperback

10 9 8   06 07 08

For my parents,
Donald and Theodora Ball

CONTENTS

For Wood ❧ ix

Selby's Secret ❧ 1

Professor Krakpott's Puzzle ❧ 10

Aunt Jetty Drops In ❧ 19

The Screaming Skull with Eyes that Glowed
with Terror ❧ 27

By the Skin of His Teeth ❧ 35

A Snake in the Grasp ❧ 43

Wild West Willy Rides Again ❧ 52

Selby's Secret Hangs in the Balance ❧ 60

Too Many Cooks ❧ 68

The Enchanted Dog ❧ 76

The Shampooed Pooch ❧ 83

Raid on Planet Kapon ❧ 90

Selby Delivers the Goods ❧ 97

Selby's Beautiful Body ❧ 105

Lucky Millions ❧ 113

A Busman's Holiday ❧ 121

Selby Sinks to New Depths ❧ 129

Bogusville Forever ❧ 137

After Wood or The Epic Log ❧ 145

About the Author ❧ 149

FOR WOOD

I just wanted to tell you something about this book. Mrs Trifle is
asleep on the lounge in front of the
fire and Dr Trifle has just gone out
the back for wood, so I'll have to
make it quick.

I've just read Selby's Secret and
I think it's pretty good. (How could it
miss, it's about me.) The thing I
think you should know is that
it's a book of short stories. But
they're the kind of stories that
are best if you read the first
one first and the second one
second and so on. Anyway, here comes
Dr Trifle with a huge log. I'd better
stop scribbling before he catches
me. Selby 🐾

SELBY'S SECRET

Selby's secret was that he was the only talking dog in Australia and — for all he knew — in the world. It wasn't a gift that he was born with. When he was young he was a perfectly ordinary barking dog. And it wasn't something that someone taught him. It just seemed to happen gradually until one day he realised that something fantastic had happened to him. Something that would change his life forever — or would it?

It all happened one evening when Selby and the Trifles were watching a TV program called *Hearthwarm Heath*. It was the story of a butler

1

who worked in a huge mansion. Selby loved the old man because he was so polite and because he knew more about everything than the lord and lady of the house. That night's episode was about an orphan girl who Basil the butler found dying in the snow. He took her into Hearthwarm Hall and looked after her but she kept stealing things and Basil had to pretend that he'd sent her away to the poorhouse — when he really had her hidden in the linen press.

Selby had watched television for years. There was never any trouble understanding what was happening. He could always figure it out just from watching. But suddenly, as he blinked back a tear for Basil and the orphan girl, he realised that he understood every word that was being said. He wasn't just looking at the pictures — he knew all the words.

Selby was so shocked that he jumped up and raced around the room saying, "Bow wow wow woof woof yip yipe yip!" — which in dog-talk meant, "I understand every word that is being said! I'm the smartest dog in the world!" — and quickly forgot about the television program.

"For heaven's sake, Selby," Mrs Trifle said. "It isn't time to eat yet. If you make so much noise, how can we hear the end of *Hearthwarm Heath*?"

"Yipe yipe bow yip yip arrrrr grrrrr!" Selby said, meaning, "Eat schmeat, I'll show you! I'll show everyone that I understand people-talk! All I have to do is learn to speak it . You'll see!"

From that moment on Selby did everything he could to learn to talk. Whenever the Trifles were out he would sit in front of the TV set repeating everything that was said. His problem was that his mouth just didn't work like a people-mouth. After a lifetime of eating dog food from a bowl and chewing Dry-Mouth Dog Biscuits, Selby's lips simply wouldn't do the things that people-lips did when they spoke. When he tried to say, "Oh bother, Basil, pass me the pepper," it came out, "Oh, gother Gasil, gas gee the gecker."

"I'm going to speak this language," Selby thought, pressing his lips against the spinning clothes drier to give himself a lip massage after practising to speak for hours, "even if it kills me.

Youch! That's hot!" he yelled, plunging his burning lips into a bucket of water. "I don't know who thought up this dreadful language but you can be sure he didn't eat Dry-Mouth Dog Biscuits. It was probably someone who could drink through a straw and do a proper pucker. In fact if I could just *say* proper pucker I'd be home and hosed."

"Proper pucker, proper pucker, proper pucker," Selby said, but it came out "hocker hucker" every time.

Gradually Selby taught himself to use his lips when he spoke and his dog-accent disappeared. When the Trifles were out of the house he spent hours in front of the hall mirror rattling off the most difficult lip-twisters he knew until, finally, he could say, "Peter Piper picked a peck of pickled peppers" so smoothly that it sounded like the rattle of a distant machine-gun.

"Oh, you perfect pooch," Selby said, and then he did a proper pucker and kissed himself in the mirror. "You're my kind of dog."

Selby's plan was simple. He would give the Trifles a Christmas present that they'd never forget. What better present could he give than to tell them his secret? His heart was bursting with joy as he pictured the wonderful scene that would follow as they stood around the fireplace, drinking egg-nog, leaning against the wall on one elbow and talking about old times and the wonderful times to come.

And what better way to spring the surprise on them than to wait till they walked in the front door on their way back from the Bogusville Christmas Dinner Charity Appeal on Christmas Eve? There, standing just inside the front door and dressed in a suit would be the new Selby; not the old throw-him-a-stick-and-see-if-he-goes-for-it Selby the pet, but the all-new talking friend-of-the-family Selby.

At last it was Christmas Eve and the Trifles were about to return from their dinner. Selby sneaked into Dr Trifle's wardrobe and got out a white shirt, a tie and one of the doctor's finest suits. With great difficulty he slipped the shirt over his head and wrapped the tie once around the collar. Then he put on the top part of the suit.

"I'll skip the dacks," Selby said, seeing that the jacket covered him from neck to tail and putting the pants back in the wardrobe. "They're a bit lacking in the number-of-legs department and, besides, the coat already covers me like a tent."

Selby stood at Mrs Trifle's dressing-table and did his hair with her hairbrush.

"If a thing's worth doing, it's worth doing right," Selby said, quoting Basil. "I could just look up from my dog-dish one day and say, 'G'day. How's it goin'?' but it really wouldn't be the same, would it?"

Just then Selby heard the Trifles' car pull into the driveway and he dashed to the loungeroom and pulled up a chair just inside the front door. He climbed up, standing on his back legs, and straightened his tie and collar.

"Don't panic, Selby," he told himself, "just remember what you're going to say and say it with feeling: 'Good evening, Madam and Sir'," he said in his best Basil-the-butler voice, "', and a very merry Christmas to you both?'"

Selby's heart raced with excitement as the Trifles crunched their way along the gravel path.

"It's on nights like this," he heard Mrs Trifle say, "that I wish we had a butler to give us an after-dinner snack and a pot of tea."

"Oh, it's so exciting! If this takes much longer I think I'll explode!" Selby squealed, looking in the mirror and deciding that — but for the long ears and hairy face — he looked quite a lot like Basil himself. "Hurry up! I can't wait any longer!"

"It's a pity," Dr Trifle said, putting his key in the lock and opening the door a crack, "that we couldn't give Selby a few things to do around the house. If he could only understand us he'd be very useful. We might even send him on errands."

"You do have a wild imagination," Mrs Trifle laughed. "A talking dog. Fancy Selby actually talking."

"Hmmmmmm."

Selby hmmmmmmed and his mind raced like a windmill.

"If we could teach the poor old thing to talk," Dr Trifle said, "we could get him to answer the telephone and take messages when we're out."

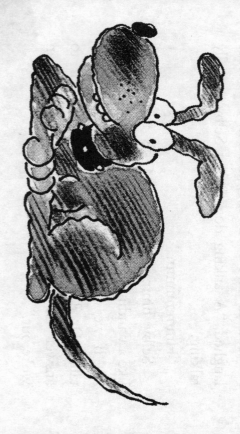

"Hmmmmmm . . . ," Selby hmmmmmmed again and suddenly his heart skipped a beat. "Poor old thing indeed," he thought. "They don't want a pet, they want a servant — and I'm about to be it! They'll have me running around like Basil the butler! Help!"

Selby thought of tearing back to the bedroom and hiding the clothes but it was too late. The door swung open and Dr and Mrs Trifle stared at him with their mouths open.

"Selby!" Mrs Trifle screamed. "What's got into you?! What do you think you're doing?!" Selby stood for an instant, frozen like a statue, and then he jumped down and raced around the room with Dr Trifle's clothes flying everywhere. And as he ran he gave the only answer he could possibly give: "Arf! Arf! Arf! Arf! Aroooooooo!" All of which in dog-talk means, "Good evening, Madam and Sir, and a very merry Christmas to you both."

And so Selby's secret remained a secret — at least for the moment.

PROFESSOR KRAKPOTT'S PUZZLE

"Choooooo!" Selby sneezed as he lay on the floor of the study watching Dr Trifle who was designing a new floral clock for the Bogusville Memorial Rose Garden. "It's not fair," he thought, "I've had this cold for a month now and it's making life very boring — very, very, extremely boring, in fact."

"What I think I'll do," Dr Trifle said absently to himself, not knowing that Selby understood every word he was saying, "is to put a water-wheel in Bogusville Creek and then connect it to the floral clock. That way the water will drive the hands of the clock! What a good idea! No winding, no electricity."

"Oh, doctor," Selby thought, "you've thought of that idea five times before but you keep forgetting it. If only I could talk to you. If only I dared."

"The mayor will be pleased as punch," Dr Trifle said, referring to Mrs Trifle, the mayor of Bogusville. "Oooops! I've forgotten to take her lunch to her."

Just then there was a knock at the door and in barged the doctor's old friend Professor Krakpott from the Department of Old and Crusty Things at the Federal University, carrying a cardboard box.

"Drop everything, Blinky," Professor Krakpott said, using Dr Trifle's old nickname and tearing the box apart. In the middle of a pile of woodshavings he found an ancient plate with a picture of a monkey on it. "This is urgent," he said. "This plate was found in the tomb of an ancient warrior in the Shandom of Feeblestan. The Shan himself has sent it to our Minister for C and B as a friendship gift."

"C and B?" Dr Trifle said, taking the plate and looking at the cracks that ran every which way and showed that the plate had once been broken and had been put back together again.

"Cakes and Biscuits," Professor Krakpott continued. "It's the Ministry for Baking Resources but everyone calls it the C and B. The Minister is about to do a big lamington deal."

"Lamington deal?" Dr Trifle said, remembering the mayor's lunch once again.

"Feeblestan is the biggest buyer of Australian lamingtons," Professor Krakpott said, putting the plate down very gently on Dr Trifle's desk. "In fact they're the only buyers of Australian lamingtons. Now it seems that they want to buy more of the wretched things. They're buttering up the C and B with the ancient plate."

"And what do you want me to do?" Dr Trifle asked.

"The Minister wants to know just what these squiggles and curlicues on the bottom mean so he can give proper thanks to the Shan."

"They're writing," Dr Trifle said, running his finger gently over them. "It's written in ancient Feeblestani."

"We know that, Blinky," Professor Krakpott said, slapping the doctor's wrist, forgetting for a minute that he wasn't at home and the doctor wasn't one of his children playing with his mashed potatoes. "The question is: what does it say?"

"I think it says, 'the great monkey of wisdom smiles on the leader'," Dr Trifle said, rubbing his wrist.

"That's what we think too, Blinky," the professor said. "But we have to make absolutely certain. We're not sure about some of these scribbly bits over here. I've got to run now so could you check the writing? I'll be back in a couple of hours."

With this, Professor Krakpott dashed out the door, nearly tripping over the sniffing Selby, and was gone as fast as he'd come.

"Yesssssss," Dr Trifle said, slowly running his finger around the plate and remembering the way he used to play with his mashed potatoes when he was a boy. "I think I'd better check my notes on this one. But the affairs of state will just have to wait a few minutes while I run the mayor's lunch down to the council chambers."

"I can't (sniff) stand it!" Selby said, holding back a sneeze when the doctor had left the house. "This is so ex-(sniff)-citing! I can't (sniff) wait to find out what the squiggles mean! I've got to know (sniff) now!"

With this Selby jumped up on the desk and climbed up the tall bookcase that stretched above it. He grabbed the box that said *Notes on Ancient Feeblestani* and was just about to climb back down when the sneeze he had held back suddenly broke loose.

"Chooooooo!" he sneezed, and the box tumbled out of his paw hitting the ancient plate and smashing it to bits. "Oh no!" he screamed. "I've savaged the saucer! I'm a done dog. Unless ... unless ..."

Selby grabbed a tube of Snap-O-Grip Pottery Plastic and quickly started gluing the pieces back together.

"This is like a jig-saw puzzle," Selby said as he finished putting the plate back together and wondered why it wasn't quite as round as it used to be. "And what's (sniff) this? I'm sure the (sniff) monkey didn't have a (sniff sniff) moustache before."

Just then Selby heard Dr Trifle returning and he quickly put the box of notes back on the bookshelf and the glue back in the desk drawer.

"Humdy hum," Dr Trifle said, running his finger around the plate again. "But what's this?

That moustachioed monkey looks just like the Minister. It's funny I didn't notice it before. And what's this? If I don't miss my guess that writing doesn't say 'the great monkey of wisdom smiles on the leader' it says 'the wise leader is a great smiling monkey'! This is an insult to the government! The Shan of Feeblestan is trying to make a monkey out of the Minister for C and B — a bigger monkey than he already is! I'd better ring the Minister and tell him to cancel his trip to Feeblestan and to stop all exports of lamingtons! But first I'll check my notes just to make sure I'm right about the translation."

"It's all my (sniff) fault," Selby thought. "I've put the plate back together wrong. This could mean war! Worse, this could mean no more lamington shipments to Feeblestan. Help!" he thought, holding back another great sneeze. "What can I do?"

Dr Trifle climbed onto the desk and stretched up on his tip-toes to reach the box of notes. And just then Selby, who was leaning against the leg of the desk for support, sneezed his great sneeze.

"Choooooool!" Selby choooooooed, and the desk shook so hard that Dr Trifle lost his grip on the box of notes and it tumbled down, smashing the plate into as many pieces as before and maybe even a few more.

"Oh no!" Dr Trifle screamed as he grabbed the Snap-O-Grip from the drawer. "I've pulverised the pot! What will I tell Professor Krakpott? He's due at any minute!"

Selby watched patiently as Dr Trifle glued the bits back together so perfectly that there weren't any cracks showing, not even the original ones.

"Well I'll be a monkey's uncle," Dr Trifle said, looking at his notes and studying the plate. "That's funny."

"What's funny?" Professor Krakpott asked as he burst into the room. "What does it say?"

"It says, 'the great monkey of wisdom smiles on the leader'," Dr Trifle said. "And the monkey doesn't have a moustache after all."

"A monkey with a moustache?" Professor Krakpott said. "Who ever heard of such a thing? Now give me that plate before you break it or something. I have to get back to the Minister straight away."

With this, Professor Krakpott snatched the plate and tore out the door.

"That was a close call," Dr Trifle said, patting Selby on the head.

"Chooooooo!" Selby sneezed as he curled up on the carpet for a snooze. "What did I (sniff) say," he thought, "about this cold making life boring?"

AUNT JETTY DROPS IN

If ever Selby almost let his secret out it was on the night of the BBBB&BC (the Bogusville Bushwalkers, Bushwhackers, Bodybuilders and Bridge Club) autumn fete. That was the night that the members got together at Bogusville Central School to raise money for the poor people of Bogusville — who were fortunately so few that, as Postie Paterson the Bogusville postman and amateur actor had once said, "They could be counted on the left hand of a right-handed butcher." It was also the last night of the Bogusville Doorknock Against Winding Roads and Potholes, only there was no one at home to collect from because everyone was out at the autumn fete — almost everyone, that is.

Selby was happy to be left at home alone that night so he could watch his favourite TV quiz show, *The Lucky Millions Quiz Quest*. Little did he know that Mrs Trifle's dreaded sister, Aunt Jetty, was tearing around the streets of Bogusville trying to collect five more dollars in her plastic collection bucket for the Doorknock so she could win the golden wishbone pin for the most money collected. Aunt Jetty's problem was there was no one to collect from.

"Drat!" Aunt Jetty said as she pounded on the door of one empty house after another. "I'll never win the pin if I can't get a fiver from someone. But who?"

Selby lay on the carpet in front of the TV answering the *Lucky Millions* questions so quickly that the contestants hadn't even buzzed their buzzers when the words were out of his mouth.

"Either these questions are getting easier," Selby said with a yawn, "or I'm getting smarter. Maybe a little of both."

"And now," screamed Larry Limelight, the compere of *Lucky Millions*, "we pause for a few messages. We'll be back with the Giant Killer Question in a moment. So don't go away."

"I'm with you, Larry," Selby said as he started to take a little cat-nap during the commercial.

Aunt Jetty was just then driving full-bore around Bunya-Bunya Crescent when she slammed on her brakes, sending her truck skidding over the kerb and into the roses in front of the Trifles' house.

"The Trifles' cardboard possum!" she screamed, starting for the front door and then remembering that her sister and Dr Trifle were out at the BBBB&BC fete along with everyone else. "They collected all that money for the Doorknock and left it in the cardboard possum piggy bank on the sideboard. If I can only get it and dash back to Doorknock headquarters before it closes I'll have the golden wishbone! Yahoo!"

Aunt Jetty tore around to the back of the house, narrowly missing a rake that was just waiting to be stepped on to pop up and hit someone on the head knocking them senseless. She quickly went to work prising open the TV room window with her Girl Guides twenty-four-in-one pocket knife and window priser.

Selby had hated Aunt Jetty since the day she told the Trifles the story of how she'd fought off a pack of African wild dogs by wading into the thick of them and thumping them on the head one by one with her walking stick. So he wasn't any happier about her when she jumped through the window where he lay napping and landed her size sixteen track-shoe on his ear.

"Ouch! Ouch! Ouch!" Selby yelled as he dashed about the room till the pain in his ear died down.

"Ouch? Ouch? Ouch?" Aunt Jetty said with a grin that spread slowly across her face like hot Vegemite. "Shouldn't you be saying 'Arf arf' or 'Bow wow' or some such doggy-talk?"

"You stepped on my ear, you great galumph," Selby said, then suddenly realised his mistake.

"Well, well, well. How do you like that, a talking dog," Aunt Jetty said, grabbing the cardboard possum and emptying it into her collection bucket. "You could be very useful indeed — very, very useful. If you don't make

22

Aunt Jetty filthy rich, then I don't know anything."

"Grrrrrr! Bow wow!" Selby snarled.

"Don't grrrrrrr me. You can talk as well as the next fellow and don't try to hide it," Aunt Jetty said. "Now tell me in the Queen's good English how you came to talk."

"Grrrrrrr!" Selby said again as he thought of the terrible fate that was in store for him.

"None of that now. Out with it!" Aunt Jetty said, raising her famous walking stick in the air. "Or I'll have your guts for garters."

Suddenly Selby lunged for Aunt Jetty's collection bucket and came out with a mouthful of dollars.

"You touch me," he warned her (though it came out "oo-utch-ee" because of the money in his mouth), "and I'll swallow the dough."

"Wait a minute. Be reasonable," Aunt Jetty said as she thought of the golden wishbone pin that she was about to lose if Selby gulped.

"Reasonable schmeasonable. One step closer and I gobble the lolly," Selby said with a slight growl.

"Okay, okay," Aunt Jetty said, dropping the walking stick, "you win."

"And," Selby added, "not a word to anyone about you-know-what."

"Okay, dog, it's a deal. Just give me back the swag. I have other fish to fry."

"Scout's honour?" Selby said, holding up his right paw and remembering that Aunt Jetty had been a Girl Guide till she was twenty-six, when they found out she was lying about her age.

"All right," Aunt Jetty said. "Scout's honour."

Selby dropped the money and watched as Aunt Jetty snapped it into the bucket. She then leaped through the window, yelling back over her shoulder as she went, "Too bad, dog, but I had my fingers crossed and it's no deal. I'll be back tomorrow and then we tell the world all about your talents," only to land squarely on the waiting rake which popped up and knocked her senseless.

"Wow," Aunt Jetty said, staggering around in circles trying to remember who she was and what she was doing wandering around in someone's backyard. "What happened? Who am I."

Selby watched from the window as she bent down and put the money back in the bucket and then turned and looked at him.

"There was something about you," she said, still seeing more stars than anything else. "Something … hmmmmmm … I've got it! You can talk, can't you?"

Selby looked straight at her and gave her his most convincing "grrrrrrr".

"Oh, sorry," Aunt Jetty said, suddenly remembering that she was due at Doorknock headquarters in five minutes and dashing away to collect the golden wishbone pin. "Isn't that funny, for a minute I thought he was a talking dog. What a riot!"

Just then Selby spun around in time to hear the Giant Killer Question and before it was fully out of Larry Limelight's mouth he had the answer: "Queen Victoria," he said calmly, "1819 to 1901. Ask us something hard for a change will you, Larry?"

THE SCREAMING SKULL WITH EYES THAT GLOWED WITH TERROR

It was just after sunset when Selby went to the bookcase and picked up the book he'd been reading called *Creepy Tales for Late-Night Enjoyment.* He knew it would be safe to do some reading without anyone seeing because Mrs Trifle had just gone out to a meeting of the council and Dr Trifle had gone to bed early.

27

"She'll be gone for hours," Selby said as he started to read the last story in the book, *The Case of the Headless Cat*, "and nothing short of a major explosion would wake Dr Trifle."

Selby curled up on the carpet and read the story and then put the book back on the bookshelf.

"Headless cat," he said with disgust. "That was no headless cat. It was just a white cat with a black head and everybody thought it was headless because they couldn't see its head at night. What a rip-off! Every story in the book was like that. There was a haunted house that wasn't haunted after all and there was a ghost that wasn't a ghost. Scary stories just aren't scary any more. I know what I'll do, I'll write my own scary story, something really creepy."

With this Selby went to the Trifles' desk and put a piece of paper in the typewriter and typed *The Screaming Skull with Eyes that Glowed with Terror* at the top.

"So much for the title," he said. "Now all I have to do is write the story. Let's see now, how will I start it? *Once upon a time there was a screaming skull* . . . No. Too much like a fairy tale.

How about: *It was a dark and stormy night* ... No, I think it's been done before. I've got it! *Suddenly the sundial struck midnight.* That's great!" he said, not really knowing what it meant but knowing that it sounded good.

Suddenly the sundial struck midnight, Selby wrote, *and a fierce wind pelted Scrunchminster Castle with rain. Lord Scrunch sat at the great oak table sipping his soup and looking at the hideous statue that his great-grandfather had stolen from a temple in Feeblestan three hundred years before.*

"Great stuff"!" Selby said as a fierce wind came up and started pelting the Trifles' house with rain. "I'm a natural writer. This is going to be easy."

All at once Lord Scrunch heard a tap tap tapping at the window, Selby continued. *And when he peered out through the old shutters there was nothing there.*

"Wow," Selby said, looking around nervously and then getting up and turning on every light he could find. "Now that's creepy the way creepy should be."

Suddenly Lord Scrunch remembered that it was his one hundredth birthday. He remembered that his

29

father and his grandfather and his great-grandfather had all died mysteriously on their one hundredth birthdays right there at the dining table at Scrunchminster Castle.

"Sheeeesh!" Selby said, looking around again. "This is almost too good."

Suddenly Lord Scrunch heard a knock knock knocking at the . . . Selby was in the middle of the sentence when he heard a tapping at the window.

"Gulp," he said, going into the lounge room and listening. "I wonder what that could be?"

The tapping came again and Selby followed its sound to the back bedroom where Dr Trifle lay sleeping. He waited for a moment and then pulled up the shade and peered into the darkness. There was nothing there.

"Probably j-just a b-branch hitting the window," he said, going back to the lounge room and turning on the TV. "I'll just put this on and then I won't feel quite so alone."

The picture on TV was of a foggy night in a graveyard. A dog barked in the background and a man with a long cape came out of the mist and gave an evil laugh. He pulled out a

30

knife and Selby's hair stood on end from head to tail.

"I j-just changed my mind about TV," Selby said, turning off the TV and turning on the radio. "Maybe a little m-m-music would be better."

"Sit back in your chairs," the voice on the radio said, "and I will tell you the story of *The Ghost's Revenge*."

"Oh no, you won't," Selby said, turning off the radio and returning to his story.

Suddenly Lord Scrunch heard a knock knock knock knocking at the back door and he sat in silence knowing that it was the screaming skull with eyes that glowed with terror. Lord Scrunch waited and soon the knocking was at the front door and a voice cried out: "Let me in. You have something of mine and I've come back to get it!"

Just then Selby heard a knock at the back door.

"It c-can't be," he said, ripping the page out of the typewriter and tearing it to shreds. "The story is coming true! Next thing you know it'll be a knocking at the front door! I can't stand it! I've got to tell Dr Trifle."

Selby dashed into the bedroom where Dr Trifle was sleeping and started barking. But the doctor was sleeping so soundly that even Selby's loudest barking couldn't wake him.

"Help!" Selby screamed in plain English. "The screaming skull with eyes that glow with terror is at the back door! Wake up!"

Selby grabbed the doctor's pillow in his teeth and shook it. For a minute the knocking stopped but then it came again — this time from the front door.

"Dr Trifle!" Selby said, shaking the sleeping man. "It's me, your faithful dog, Selby! I can talk! I don't care who knows it now! Just wake up and take care of the screaming skull and I'll be your servant for life!"

Dr Trifle stopped snoring for a second and then rolled over and started snoring again.

"This is hopeless," Selby said, tearing out of the bedroom with the pillowcase in his teeth. "You can't depend on humans. I'll have to take matters into my own paws. And the only way to deal with this monster is to fight fire with fire."

"Let me in! You have something of mine and

I've come back to get it!" the voice outside yelled in the wind.

Selby pulled a high stool to the front door and then climbed on top of it and put the pillowcase over his head.

"Good," he thought. "I can see through the pillowcase. I'll just open the door and when I see the skull I'll leap at it and scare it to death — or scare it anyway."

"Let me in!" the voice outside the door said again; and the knocking got louder and louder.

"I'll let you in," Selby thought as his heart pounded like a bass drum. "I'll let you in all right!"

With this Selby flung open the door and with a mighty "*Aaaaaaaaaaggggggggghhhhhhh!*" jumped into the darkness, clearing Mrs Trifle's head by centimetres, and ran across the front lawn and into the bushes.

"That's odd," Dr Trifle said as he stepped into the lounge 0.0room rubbing his eyes. "I wonder what's got into Selby. He seems to have got stuck in a pillowcase or something, poor old thing."

"I don't know," Mrs Trifle said. "I just came back to get the bag you took from the car this afternoon. It has all the papers I need for the meeting and my house keys as well. You certainly are a sound sleeper. I've knocked on every door and window in the place."

BY THE SKIN OF HIS TEETH

Selby's first problem was a terrible toothache. His second problem was that somehow he had to tell Dr and Mrs Trifle he had a toothache without coming right out with it in plain English and giving away his secret — a secret that he was going to keep even if it killed him.

"Look," Mrs Trifle said to her husband. "Look at the cute way Selby can curl his lip back. Isn't that clever."

"Clever schmever," Selby thought. "I've got a toothache you silly sausage. Don't look at the lip, look at the teeth."

Finally, when Selby's lip was almost as sore from curling it back as his tooth was, he put a paw to his jaw and let out a sound like a werewolf howling at a full moon.

"My goodness," Dr Trifle said, looking up from the book he was reading, *The Inventor's Guide to Fast-Moving Cam Shafts and Water-Driven Floral Clocks*, "I do believe Selby has a toothache."

"No kidding, Sherlock," Selby muttered under his breath. "You're lovely people, both of you, but sometimes you forget that we dogs have our problems too. Now how about doing something about it?"

"The poor old thing," Mrs Trifle said, looking at Selby's swollen gums. "I'll take him to the vet tomorrow and have the tooth pulled."

Vet? Pulled? The words raced through Selby's brain like a two-headed goose through clover. "When *they* have a toothache do *they* go to a vet and have it pulled? Not on your tonsils," Selby thought. "They go to a proper tooth-carpenter and have it fixed. But when it's a poor dumb animal," he thought, knowing that there was nothing dumb about this animal, "they'd have his tooth pulled as quick as they could blow their noses. Oh, spare me. I'll have to think of something . . . ."

That afternoon when Mrs Trifle was at a special meeting of the Possum Protection Committee and the doctor was in his workshop making a model of the floral clock at the Bogusville Memorial Rose Garden, Selby sneaked to the phone and dialled Rita Houndstooth, the town dentist.

"With a name like Houndstooth," Selby said, "she ought to know a little about my problem."

"Hello," the voice on the other end of the phone said, "dentist's surgery. Dr Houndstooth here, can I help you?"

"This is Dr Trifle of Bunya–Bunya Crescent," Selby said, putting on his best imitation of the doctor's voice. "Do you treat dogs?"

There was a deathly silence on the phone and then Dr Houndstooth said, "Good heavens no. Is this a joke?"

"Joke schmoke," Selby thought, trying to stay calm. "Do you mean to say that if my dog had a toothache, you wouldn't treat him?"

"Oh!" Dr Houndstooth said, and she let out a great scream of a laugh. "I thought you asked me if I *eat* dogs. Oh, *treat* dogs . . . well let me see. I've never treated a dog before but I'll have a go. I mean they have teeth like everybody else, don't they?"

"They do indeed," Selby said, drawing in a deep breath as a stab of pain shot through his jaw.

"He doesn't bite, does he?" Dr Houndstooth asked.

"Bite? Certainly not," Selby said. "I can assure you that Selby is the most mild-mannered dog on God's green earth. He's a perfect gentle — er . . . gentledog."

"Well then, bring him in by all means," Dr Houndstooth said, wondering if gentledog was one word or two.

"Mrs Trifle will be bringing him in," Selby said. "But there's just one problem. Mrs Trifle isn't quite herself these days."

"Then who exactly is she?" Dr Houndstooth asked.

"Well I'm not sure," Selby said. "It's just that she's under so much pressure because of her work that she often comes out with some very strange things. So when she brings Selby in, just agree with everything she says."

Selby slammed down the phone, dashed to the typewriter and wrote a letter:

Dear Dr and Mrs Trifle,

We are pleased to announce a new service. We now offer dentistry for dogs. If your dog has teeth problems, bring him to us.

Yours sincerely, Rita Houndstooth

That evening Mrs Trifle found Selby's letter tucked under the front door and the next day she and Selby were off to the dentist's surgery.

"Your letter arrived just in time," Mrs Trifle said. "We were just about to take Selby to the vet to have his tooth pulled. Maybe you can save it."

"Yes, yes, Mrs Trifle," Dr Houndstooth said, sitting her down in a comfortable chair and handing her a seven-year-old copy of *You and Your Teeth* magazine. "You just have a good rest and leave Selby to me."

Selby lay back innocently in the dentist's chair, looking at the mobile overhead.

"Vet," he thought as Dr Houndstooth started to put him to sleep with gas. "Can you imagine?

They were going to send me to the vet to have my tooth pulled. This is more like it."

A warm and wonderful feeling spread through his body as the gas started to work and

Selby felt just a little like whistling the theme song from *The Lucky Millions Quiz Quest*. Then, suddenly he was awake and his tooth was fixed. He lay back in a happy daze and, without thinking, began to sing:

"Love that money madness,
See those dollars drifting down,
Sing away your troubles,
  Hang upside down."

"What was that?" the dentist said, spinning around like a windmill in a cyclone. "Who said that?"

Selby realised his mistake and gave her a blank stare.

"It was you, wasn't it?" the dumbfounded dentist said, staring at Selby's innocent face.

It was a stealthy paw that crept out and slowly turned on the radio that stood on the bench next to the dentist's chair. Slowly, he turned the sound up and then just as slowly he pulled his paw back under the dental bib.

"Oh," Dr Houndstooth said with some relief. "I must have left the radio on. For a second I thought you — a dog — were actually singing. What a scream!"

"That was a close one," Selby thought as he climbed down from the chair and headed for the waiting room. "Any closer and everyone would have had something to scream about."

A SNAKE IN THE GRASP

"This reptile cage must be fixed at once," Mrs Trifle said to Postie Paterson, Bogusville's postman, amateur actor and keeper of reptiles at the Bogusville Zoo. "It's simply not fit for any sort of animal — not even a snake."

"But who will look after Bazza the boa constrictor while I fix the cage?" Postie asked.

"I will," said Mrs Trifle. "Put him in a box and bring him round to my house this afternoon. Make it early though because Dr Trifle and I have to go out at about three."

Just before three o'clock Postie Paterson arrived at the Trifles' house with a big box and put it down on the carpet next to where Selby lay, pretending to sleep.

"Bazza loves opera," Postie told Mrs Trifle. "He was born in the trunk of a touring opera company, The Western Plains Bel Canto, and they used him in an opera when he was little."

"Not a singing part, I trust," Mrs Trifle said to be funny, knowing that animals couldn't sing — but not knowing that Selby could not only talk, he could sing the complete opera *Cleopatra and the Asp*, which he used to play on the stereo when the Trifles were out of the house.

"No, of course he didn't sing. He was just a prop. He was in an opera called *Cleopatra and the Asp*," Postie Paterson said, not seeing Selby's ears shoot up. "You see, Cleopatra committed suicide by having a poisonous snake bite her. In the opera the soprano used to pick Bazza up, pretend he bit her and then sing to him for half an hour as she died. Of course boa constrictors aren't poisonous so they could use the same soprano night after night. Even now when I play *Cleopatra and the Asp* Bazza goes limp all over and I swear there are tears of joy in his eyes."

"So how did a talented snake like this end up in the Bogusville Zoo?" Mrs Trifle asked.

"He outgrew the part," Postie said. "He got so heavy that even the baritone couldn't lift him. The opera company was touring out here at the time so they just had to leave him."

"Speaking of leaving," Mrs Trifle said, "we have to go right away. I hope Bazza will be safe there in his box."

"Perfectly," Postie said. "Nothing to worry about. I'll get back to the zoo and fix the cage. I'll pick up Bazza tomorrow."

"Snakes," Selby said, peering in the air holes in the top of Bazza's box when Postie Paterson and the Trifles had left the house. "Sheeeeeeesh! They give me the creeps. But," he added, "Bazza must be special to have played lead snake in *Cleopatra and the Asp*."

And Selby would have left it at that if he hadn't suddenly thought of the last episode of his favourite TV nature show, *Go and Grab 'Em*, with Flash Finlay, who could outrun most wild animals and trick the rest into letting him catch them. In that show, Flash Finlay was covered from head to toe in carpet snakes.

"If snakes were warm and had fur," he had said at the end of his program, "people would forget about keeping cats and dogs as pets and keep a snake instead. So until next week let me leave you with this suggestion: snuggle a snake tonight."

"Want to hear some music?" Selby said, putting the first record of *Cleopatra and the Asp* on the stereo and then peering down the air holes in the box again to see if there were tears of joy in Bazza's eyes but not seeing any. "Blimey," Selby added as his own eyes got a little watery. "Such a small box for a big snake. No wonder you're not having much fun."

Selby opened the top of the box and looked straight into Bazza's sad eyes.

"Oh, Baz," Selby said, "don't look at me like that. You're breaking my heart. Come on out of there you big sausage," he added, tipping Bazza out onto the carpet like so many metres of rope.

Selby lay back listening to the heavenly strains of *Cleopatra and the Asp* and thinking how proud Flash Finlay would have been if he knew that one of *Go and Grab 'Em's* greatest fans had taken his advice and was snuggling a snake. All of which might have been perfectly okay if there hadn't been a cold wind blowing under the door.

"I'll tell you what, Baz," Selby said, still looking for tears of joy in the snake's eyes but still not seeing any, "how about doing something useful like blocking that draught."

Selby struggled to lift Bazza with his front paws without success. He then put his head under the snake and started to lift and push him in the direction of the door.

"Phew!" Selby said, struggling to push the great limp Bazza to where the draught was blowing in. "No (*puff*) wonder you had to (*puff puff*) retire. You weigh a (*puff*) tonne."

Suddenly the record finished and the stereo turned off and just as suddenly the now-not-so-limp Bazza wound himself slowly around Selby's neck with his other end winding around Selby's legs.

"Ah — er — Bazza," Selby said, trying to unwind the snake but finding that he was winding even faster, "would you mind stopping that?"

Selby flipped his head around and untangled Bazza from his neck, only to find that the snake's other end had taken two turns around his middle.

"If (gasp) I can only (gasp) get to the stereo and put on the next (gasp) record," said Selby, gripped by snake and panic.

But Bazza was too heavy and Selby was stopped dead in his tracks next to the telephone.

"I've got it!" Selby said, snatching the phone and dialling the *Go and Grab 'Em* show.

"*Go and Grab 'Em*," the voice on the other end of the phone said. "Flash Finlay speaking."

"I took your advice, Flash," Selby said, "and snuggled a snake."

"Good for you," Flash Finlay said cheerily, "that's the spirit. Thank you for calling —"

"Wait!" Selby interrupted. "I've got a bit of a problem."

"And haven't we all these days," Flash said.

"Well my problem's a bit (gasp) different from most," Selby said as Bazza took another turn around his waist. "You see, the snake I (gasp) chose to snuggle is a boa constrictor and he's squeezing me."

"No, no, no," Flash said. "He's not squeezing you —"

"He blinkin' well is, you know —" Selby said.

"No, he's *constricting*. That's what boa constrictors are all about."

"Squeezing, constricting, what's the difference?" Selby said. "He's wrapped himself around my waist and he won't let go."

"Do you realise that a full-grown boa constrictor is capable of reducing a medium-size mammal to one large mouthful?" Flash said.

"Why, I was on an expedition to the westernmost reaches of the Amazon a couple of years ago and I had with me my favourite tracker-dog. Next thing I knew the dog had strayed from the path and —"

"All right! All right!" Selby screamed.

"Don't you want to hear what happened to my dog?"

"No! Just ... tell me ... how to get this ... monster off me," Selby said, just barely able to choke out his words.

"I don't know," Flash said. "That's not my department. I suppose you could try grabbing him with both hands and unwinding him."

"And what if I don't have ... (growk) ... any (screek) ... (glug)," Selby said as Bazza squeezed his throat. Now all Selby could do was make a bubbling, scraping sound and a high-pitched scream followed by another scream and another.

Slowly Bazza began to relax his grip, and Selby realised that his screams sounded just like the song of the dying soprano in *Cleopatra and the Asp.* He kept screaming and singing till the snake had let go and lay limp at his feet on the carpet — this time with real tears of joy in his eyes.

"Hello! Hello!" said Flash Finlay's voice on the dangling telephone as Selby picked it up again. "Are you all right there?"

"Quite good, wouldn't you say," Selby said, calmly pushing Bazza back into his box, "considering I haven't sung that part of *Cleopatra and the Asp* for over a month."

WILD WEST WILLY RIDES AGAIN

The day of the Greater Bogusville Easter Egg Rolling Contest was a day that Selby feared and hated more than any other day of the year. It was the day when all the children of Bogusville came to the Trifles' house to roll Easter eggs across the front lawn with their noses. It was also the day that Aunt Jetty's dreadful son Willy came to make Selby's life a living hell.

"Here he is, Selby!" Mrs Trifle said as her sister's truck pulled up and Willy jumped out dressed in his cowboy outfit and twirling a lasso over his head. "And he wants to play with you before the egg rolling contest."

"Crikey!" Selby thought, jumping to his feet. "I overslept. I'd better nip out through the back door and make myself scarce for the day."

It had all started a few years before when Willy had taken one look at Selby and jumped on him, digging his heels into Selby's ribs and yelling: "Ride 'em cowboy! Wild West Willy's come to town!" Poor Selby couldn't walk for a week.

Every year since then Selby had tried to escape from Willy. But every year he was caught and ridden around the house like a wild bull at a rodeo.

"This year," Selby said, slipping out the back door and heading full-speed for the bush, "is going to be different. Wild West Willy won't see me for dust."

No sooner were the words out of his mouth than Willy's lasso caught him around the neck and brought him down like a stray calf.

"Got you, Horsey!" Willy yelled and a chill went through Selby's scalp that didn't finish till it reached the tip of his tail. "Now get up! We're going to play cowboys!"

For the next hour Selby was chased, ridden, lassoed and tied up until he was so exhausted that he had to stand perfectly still with his legs apart just to stay on his feet.

"Hold it right there, Horsey! I like it when you stand still like that," Willy said as he hurtled through the air and landed squarely on Selby's back, sending him crashing to the ground.

"Whoooooooooooppppeeeeee!" Willy yelled.

"Crumbs," Selby sighed as Wild West Willy wrapped a rope round and round his legs. "What did I ever do to deserve this?"

"And now I'll try out my new branding iron," Willy said, pulling a red hot poker with three "W"s on the end out of the barbecue.

"Heaven help me!" Selby thought. "The kid's actually going to brand me! If that thing touches me I'm a goner!"

Selby was just about to scream out, "Stop it, you idiot!" in plain English when Aunt Jetty came bounding round the corner.

"Willy!" she yelled. "Stop that this instant! You'll miss the beginning of the egg rolling contest! The children are all waiting at the start. Hurry!"

54

"Oh, boy. Oh, boy," Willy said, dropping the branding iron and breaking into a run. "I'm going to win! I'm going to win the egg rolling contest again!"

"You always win, dear," Aunt Jetty said, unwinding the rope from Selby's legs. "Hmmmmmmm," she said, giving him a puzzled look. "There's something strange about you. I seem to remember something … yes, now I remember. You talked. That was it! I had a dream that you talked in plain English. Isn't that a riot? Ha!"

"Some day I'll show *you* a riot, you big nit," Selby thought, struggling to his feet as Aunt Jetty dashed off to watch the start of the egg rolling contest.

"Remember the rules," Mrs Trifle said to the line of children who waited on their hands and knees on the wet grass. "You must push your egg straight across the lawn with your nose. No hands. And mind the puddles. The first one across the finish line wins the pavlova."

"Oh, boy," Willy said, pushing his way into the middle of the starting line. "I won last year and the year before and I'm going to win again this year. So everybody out of my way or else!"

Selby stumbled around the corner just as the bell rang and the girls and boys started off across the lawn.

"Clear off!" Willy said as he knocked three boys over and made his way to the middle of the pack.

"That's the way, Willy!" Aunt Jetty cheered, jumping up and down on the sidelines. "You're faster than them! You can beat them!"

"Get out of here!" Willy said in a low voice to another boy and pushed past, until he was just behind the leader, Sally Rudge.

"Out of my way, Sally," Willy said savagely. "I'm coming through."

"You are not," Sally said, nudging her egg quickly forward with her nose. "I'm faster than you and I'm going to win."

"I'm warning you," Willy said. "You win, and you're going to be sorry. If you win — you'll lose. So out of the way!"

A silence fell over the crowd, except for the screams of "Get her, Willy! Get her!" from Aunt Jetty. No one but his mother wanted to see

56

Willy win the race — and now there was only Sally and a few metres of ground between him and the finish line.

Willy closed in on Sally and then accidentally-on-purpose fell on her legs. Sally crashed down on her egg, smashing it.

"You ruined my egg!" Sally screamed as Willy passed. "That's not fair!"

"I didn't touch your silly egg," Willy said. "Don't be a spoilsport."

Now, with nothing between Willy and victory, Selby's anger finally got the best of him. He raced to the starting line and began pushing a spare Easter egg across the lawn at a speed that only a short, angry dog could manage.

"I'll beat that kid!" Selby said, digging his paws into the wet ground. "I've got to beat him!"

A cheer went up from the sidelines as he closed in on the cowboy. He dodged the puddles like a slalom skier dodging flags, but soon there was silence again, for although he had passed everyone else Willy was just centimetres from the finish line.

As he came up behind Willy, Selby whispered in a tone that only Willy could hear:

"Hey, brat! Look behind you. There's a wild stallion on your heels!"

Willy was so startled that he turned around and Selby bumped against him and knocked him head first into the biggest, muddiest puddle on the lawn and then shot by and crossed the finish line.

"That's not fair!" Willy yelled, standing up and looking like a huge chocolate icecream cone. "Horsey cheated. He talked to me. I won the race. I want the pavlova."

Fortunately for Selby, no one — not even Aunt Jetry — believed Willy when he said that Selby had talked to him. Unfortunately, when it came to giving out the prize, Mrs Trifle gave it to Willy.

"Selby won the race," she said. "But we can't very well give a dog a pavlova. It would only make him sick."

"I'd eat every blinking piece of it," Selby thought, "just to keep that brat from getting it."

With this Selby jumped up on the table where the pavlova was and stood over it, perfectly still. Willy saw him out of the corner of his eye and suddenly the sight of Selby standing

58

still like a brahman bull in a chute ready to be ridden made something in him snap.

"Hold still, Horsey!" Wild West Willy yelled, forgetting about the pavlova and jumping towards Selby's waiting back. "Ride 'em cowboy! Yaaaaaaahhhhooooooool!"

But before the "hoooooooo" was out of his mouth — while he was still hurtling through the air on a beeline for his victim — Selby stepped neatly out of the way and Willy landed smack in the middle of the pavlova.

"Oh, sorry, brat," Selby whispered in Willy's ear. "Better luck next year," and off he went to watch *The Lucky Millions Quiz Quest*.

SELBY'S SECRET HANGS IN THE BALANCE

"Selby's reading the newspaper!" screamed Barnstorm Billy, dreaded son of Aunt Jetty and brother of Selby's old enemy Wild West Willy.

"Selby's only a dog," Dr Trifle said patiently, "and dogs can't read."

"He *is* reading!" Barnstorm Billy yelled. "I saw his eyes moving. Come quick!"

Selby lay on top of a copy of the *Bogusville Banner*, reading the ad for the Windy Scrub Roving Big Top Circus, which had just come to Bogusville. The ad said:

SEE THE FLYING FERGUSONS' HIGHWIRE SPECTACULAR

FEATURING BARNEY THE BALANCING MIRACLE DOG

WITH HIS PAWS OF STEEL. Also See Our Lions, Tigers,

Elephants And Camels – One Hump And Two.

"Paws of steel," Selby, who was always interested in talented dogs, muttered. "Wow! That really sends shivers up my spine. I'd love to see that act."

"Come quickly, uncle!" Barnstorm Billy yelled, dragging Dr Trifle into the lounge room. "He's reading. Look!"

Selby lay perfectly still on the newspaper with his eyes closed and pretended to sleep.

"He's not reading, Billy," Dr Trifle said politely. "He's only sleeping. He often sleeps on the newspaper."

"But he *was* reading. I know a reading dog when I see one," Billy protested. "And I saw one!"

"Nobody's going to believe you, kid," Selby thought. "And thank goodness for that."

Selby pretended to sleep so well that soon he was really asleep. When he awoke it was evening and there was no one in the house.

"This is great," Selby thought. "The Trifles are probably driving the brat back to Aunt Jetty's house. I think I'll just nip over to the Windy Scrub Circus to check out Barney the Balancing Miracle Dog."

Selby waited behind the circus tent till he saw a trainer leading three elephants and two camels into the back entrance.

"I'll just sneak in with this lot," he thought as he trotted along into the darkness beside one of the elephants, "and no one will notice. There are times when it pays not to be human."

Just then a strong pair of hands reached out and grabbed him.

"Hey, Eliot!" the voice said. "I've got the dog."

"What dog is that, Ian?" another voice answered.

"The one from the agency. He's replacing Barney the Balancing Miracle Dog."

"What happened to Barney?"

"He fell off the wire. Broke all four legs. Luckily he hit a camel on the way down."

"One hump or two?"

"Two, fortunately. One hump and he would have been history," the man said. "Quick. Help me get him into this basket. He's on right now."

Before Selby could bite or scratch or even scream out in plain English, he found himself in an open basket being lifted by a rope to the very top of the gigantic tent. Music played and the crowd cheered as the basket reached the tiny platform at one end of the highwire. Then Fred Ferguson, of the Flying Fergusons, tipped him out of the basket. Selby took one look down and held tight to Fred as the crowd went quiet and a drum roll started.

"Get out there, dog," Fred said in a loud whisper as he pulled the clinging Selby loose and pushed him towards the wire.

"No way!" Selby thought, grabbing a long balancing pole in his teeth to make it harder for Fred to push him. "I'll just play dumb till they realise their mistake. There's no way I'm going out on that wire."

"They've sent us another hopeless dog, Frieda," Fred Ferguson whispered across to the woman on the platform at the other end of the wire. "What can we do?"

"You could give him a good shove," Frieda suggested. "But it's no good if he doesn't feel up to it. He'll only fall and make a mess and put everyone off their fairy-floss."

"Crikey!" Selby thought, swallowing hard and covering his eyes with one paw. "Put them off their fairy-floss! How do I get into these things?"

Just then there was a yell from the audience. "It's him, uncle!" Barnstorm Billy shouted. "It's Selby! He reads newspapers and he does circus tricks! Look!"

"Oh, no, they've brought the brat to the circus," Selby said, peering down into the darkness.

And in the silence, Selby heard Dr Trifle say, "You're right. It *is* Selby! But it can't be. Selby's no acrobat. Besides, he's too old to walk a highwire."

"I'm a goner," Selby thought. "If I don't walk the wire the Trifles will know it's me. They'll believe Barnstorm Billy. They'll know I was reading the newspaper. My secret will be out and . . . and . . . and then what? They'll be happy at first. I'll be welcomed into the family fold and I'll sit at the table at dinnertime. But then what? Then it will be: 'Selby, dear, do you mind answering the phone while we're out?' and 'Selby, dear, would you mind popping down to the shops?' and 'Today we're going to show you how to use the lawnmower'. Gulp. I don't want to answer the telephone or do the shopping or mow the blinking lawn! What do they think I am, their slave? I'll have to go out on that wire. I'll have to convince them it's not me up here."

With this, Selby put one foot out on the wire and the crowd roared.

"Where's that bloomin' two-humped camel?" Selby thought, putting another foot onto the wire and then another. "One more foot on the wire and there will be no turning back. I think I can, I think I can . . ."

Fear gripped Selby's head like a vice as his fourth foot stepped onto the wire and sweat began to drip from his chin.

"I'll show them," he thought as he began his walk across the wire.

Halfway across, Frieda motioned with her hands for him to stand on his hind legs.

"You've got to be kidding, lady," Selby muttered to himself. "I was born with four legs and I'm going to use every one of them."

Just then Fred Ferguson jumped out on the wire and Selby lost his balance and dropped his balancing pole into the darkness below, narrowly missing a two-humped camel. He teetered back and forth on his hind legs as the audience screamed and Barnstorm Billy cried out, "Goody goody, he's going to fall!"

Then, with a sudden burst of energy born of terror, Selby dashed along the wire on his hind legs and leaped into Frieda's waiting arms.

On his way down in the basket the whole audience was on its feet cheering and stamping and Selby's fear turned to pride. He stood on his hind legs and bowed to the roaring crowd.

When he reached the ground he tore into the crowd to avoid the trainers and made his escape through a hole in the tent. As he passed Barnstorm Billy and the Trifles he heard Mrs Trifle say: "What a dog! What a brilliant and talented dog! He looks like Selby but he can't be."

"I wouldn't count on it," Selby said when he was safely at home lying in front of the TV watching *The Lucky Millions Quiz Quest*. "I may not have paws of steel but I've got more talent in my big toe than Billy has in his whole body."

TOO MANY COOKS

In general, Selby liked his fellow dogs. But Aunt Jetty's dog, Crusher, was nasty and pushy and — what was worse — was staying with the Trifles for the day.

"You're probably not to blame," Selby said to Crusher, knowing that Crusher didn't understand any sort of people-talk or even dog-talk for that matter. "Anyone who lives in the same house as Aunt Jetty and her dreadful sons deserves a medal."

But within fifteen minutes, Crusher had pushed Selby out of the way and gobbled all his food and then chased him around the house nipping at his heels until Selby fell exhausted in a heap on the lounge-room carpet. To make matters worse, Crusher fell on top of him like a sack of potatoes.

"All right, all right," Selby said. "Get up. You win. You're the boss. Just go away and leave me in peace."

Crusher just lay there for a few minutes and when he did get up it was to give Selby another good chomp and then start chasing him around the house again.

"Stop it now, you two," Dr Trifle said as he stood in the kitchen making Mrs Trifle's favourite dessert, Marshmallow Cream Cake, as a special birthday surprise. "If you run around like that the cake will fall. You can play some more after I go out."

"Crumbs," Selby thought as he curled up at the doctor's feet. "Please don't leave me alone with this savage. Stay here and protect me."

But soon the cake was finished and Dr Trifle put it on the kitchen counter next to an open window to cool. Then he left the house and the chase was on again.

"Heeeeeeellllp!" Selby screamed as he tore through the dining room for the twenty-seventh time, his hind legs bruised black and blue from Crusher's nipping. "Somebody help me, please! I can't keep this up forever!"

"I know what I'll do," Selby thought as he tore over the top of the piano and then under the lounge. "One advantage in being a talking, thinking, just-plain-clever dog instead of a brute like Crusher is I can open and close doors. I'll just slip out the front door and lock Crusher in."

Selby darted out the door, but before he could close it Crusher burst out, knocking Selby into the dirt. The door flew open, hit the side of the house and then bounced closed with a slam. "Crikey! Now we're both locked out!" Selby thought as he ran around and around the garden sprinkler and then in and out of the bushes with Crusher nipping his tail all the while. "My only chance is to jump in an open window."

Selby tore around the house but the only open window was the kitchen window, which was too high.

"I've got it! Ouch!" Selby screamed as he saw his escape and Crusher nipped his tail all

70

at the same moment. And with this he suddenly turned and ran straight at Crusher, letting out a bloodcurdling scream that stopped the brute in his tracks. Selby then leaped up on Crusher's back with one bound and through the kitchen window with another. All of which would have been a perfect escape if he hadn't landed smack in the middle of the Marshmallow Cream Cake, sending bits of it flying everywhere.

"Oh, no! I've crushed the cream cake!" Selby said, licking himself off and then quickly cleaning up the mess. "I'd better make another one fast before the Trifles return."

Selby raced through the recipe, adding cups of this and teaspoons of that, while Crusher ran around the house barking to be let in.

"It's all your fault, you oaf!" Selby said, slamming the window just as a gust of wind blew in and turned the page of the recipe book.

"Hmmmmmmmm," he said, looking back at the book but not knowing he was reading a different recipe. *Add one cup of your hottest curry powder and blend well*, he read. "That's strange. Oh, well, it must be right."

71

Selby grabbed a one-cup size packet of Fire Eater's Triple Hot Curry Powder and threw it into the mix. He gave it a quick stir and then poured it into a cake tin and put it in the oven to bake.

Selby took the cake out of the oven. It was perfect. He turned it onto a plate and was just finishing the icing when he heard the Trifles' car pull into the driveway. Quickly Selby put the cake in front of the window where the other cake had been.

He opened the window and was scraping the cake tin clean with his paw when the Trifles reached the front door. The key turned in the lock. Selby thrust his crumb-laden paw into his mouth, intending to swallow the evidence.

"I-yi-yi-yi-yi-aooooooooeeeeee!" he shrieked as he tore past the Trifles who were just coming in.

He ran to the garden sprinkler and put his mouth over the nozzle, drinking every drop that came out of it.

"That … (gulp) … is … (gulp) … the … (gulp) … hottest … (gulp) … Marshmallow

Cream Cake . . . I've ever tasted!" he mumbled. "I've got to keep the Trifles from eating it. One big bite could set them on fire."

All through Mrs Trifle's birthday dinner, Selby tried to think of ways of getting rid of the Marshmallow Cream Cake as Crusher chased him around the house. But it was no use, the cake stayed on the table in full view.

"I've got to warn them," Selby thought, ignoring a bite on the ear from Crusher. "I think I'll have to come right out with it in plain English. It will be the end of my secret — and the end of me — but I have to do it. I can't let them eat the cake."

Selby turned and faced the Trifles. Looking deep into their eyes he cleared his throat.

"I do believe Selby is trying to tell us something," Dr Trifle said to Mrs Trifle. "Do you suppose he wants a piece of Marshmallow Cream Cake?"

"I —" Selby started. "I —" He cleared his throat again and thought how lucky he was to live with such kind and generous people, people who would offer their own Marshmallow Cream Cake to a not-so-dumb animal like

73

himself. A tear came into his eye and he opened his mouth to speak again.

Just then, with the Trifles watching Selby, Crusher saw his chance. He jumped up on the table and gobbled the whole Marshmallow Curry and Cream Cake with one big gobble, not leaving the tiniest crumb on the plate.

"Oooooooo-bow-bow-wow-wow-yiiiiiii!" Crusher barked as he ran straight through the

screen door into the garden, and began drinking the sprinkler dry.

"This is all very odd," Mrs Trifle said, forgetting about Selby and looking at where the cake had been. "I wonder what got into Crusher?"

"A whole cup of Fire Eater's Triple Hot Curry Powder," Selby thought as he lay down on the carpet to get some rest at last. "And he deserved every speck of it."

THE ENCHANTED DOG

"Oh look," said Mrs Trifle, who was reading the latest copy of the *Sisters of Limelight Every-Two-Weekly Newsletter*, "the Bogusville Stagestompers are doing a play called *The Enchanted Dog* and they need a dog for the title role. I think I'll take Selby to the audition to see if he can get the part."

Selby's ears shot up.

"I've always wanted to act," he thought. "Ever since I did my highwire act at the circus I've been addicted to applause. Now I can't get enough of it."

That afternoon Mrs Trifle took Selby to the Bogusville Bijou where the author and director of the play, Melanie Mildew, who was also the gardener at the Bogusville Memorial Rose Garden when she wasn't writing and directing plays, was just starting the first rehearsal.

"Will he sit when you ask him to?" Melanie asked Mrs Trifle.

"Yes, of course," Mrs Trifle answered.

"And will he come when he's called?"

"Well yes, I think so."

"He'll be perfect," Melanie said. "Just leave him with us."

"It doesn't sound like a very demanding part," Selby thought. "But it'll have to do."

"Attention everyone," Melanie said, clapping her hands above her head. "We have a dog. We can begin. Now let me tell you about the play. It's about a bullock driver who comes to a sheep station which is owned by three sisters who are really witches. They need a dog to drive their sheep. So they invite the bullocky in for dinner, feed him some pawpaw that they've cast a spell on and then play some music that turns him into a sheepdog."

"Great stuff!" thought Selby, who was really getting into the swing of things.

"The big scene is when the bullocky — that's you," Melanie said to Postie Paterson, "tries to break the spell by dancing *The Dance of Darkness*."

"Why does he want to break the spell?" Selby wondered. "What's so bad about being a dog?"

"What you do is this," Melanie said. "You eat the pawpaw and then stagger out of the house into the moonlight and fall behind that rock over there. Selby will be hiding there and all you have to do is push him out into the spotlight while you change into the dog suit. When you've got the suit on, you call Selby back behind the rock and then we cut the spotlight and you do *The Dance of Darkness*. The stage will be very dark and you will look just like a real dog dancing around. Okay? So *The Dance of Darkness* breaks the spell and the three sisters turn into emus and go running off. End of play. Everybody got it?"

"Let's see," Selby thought. "First I sit still behind the rock. Then I stand in the spotlight.

Then I go back behind the rock and sit some more. Not a great part but I'll see what I can do with it."

"All right, then," Melanie said. "Places everyone. Let's give it a run-through."

On opening night a full house watched in silence as the Stagestompers performed the first act of *The Enchanted Dog* and Selby waited behind the rock for his big moment. The magic of the play began to bring out the actor in him and he felt his heart throb when Postie Paterson gagged on the enchanted pawpaw and staggered towards him.

Not waiting to be pushed, Selby leaped out from behind the rock as soon as Postie fell behind it. He jumped into the spotlight and stood there on his hind legs, turning from side to side so the audience could get a good look at him.

"This is wonderful!" Selby thought, and the excitement of the moment surged through him sending shivers of delight up his spine.

Then from behind the rock he heard Postie Paterson whisper: "Pssssssssst! Here doggy. That's enough."

But instead of just walking back behind the rock as the spotlight went off, Selby leaped high in the air, jumping over the rock and hitting Postie squarely on the back as he bent down to put on the pants part of the dog suit. Postie went down with a crash, hitting his head on the floor.

"Postie!" Selby whispered, risking giving away his secret. "Are you okay?"

But there was no answer and in a moment a murmur rose from the audience as they wondered what would happen next.

"You are caught in our web of darkness," one of the witches said for the third time. "You will never escape from us now."

The murmur soon grew to a mass of whispers and then Selby called out in a voice that sounded just like the postman's: "I will break your spell forever. I will dance *The Dance of Darkness* and be forever free."

Selby danced out in the half-light of the stage, whirling and twirling as the audience fell silent again. He leaped about as the music grew louder, feeling its beat flow through him. The audience gasped at the sight of the shadowy

dog-figure and from the back of the stalls someone cried out, "Brilliant!" and another, "What acting! What dancing!"

Selby danced faster and faster; first on all fours, then on his hind legs and then leaping from leg to leg at blinding speed. Suddenly — just as the music stopped and the curtain began to fall — Selby saw Postie Paterson begin to come to. He leaped back behind the rock just as the house lights came on. The audience stood up and shouted "Bravo! Bravo!" and Melanie

81

Mildew dashed across the stage and threw her arms around Postie Paterson who had just staggered out from behind the rock.

"You were fabulous!" she cried. "What a dancer! And that dog suit was perfect! You looked more like a dog than Selby!"

"Don't let it go to your head," Selby thought, feeling more proud of himself by the moment.

"But ... but," sputtered Postie Paterson, holding his aching head with both hands, "I can't remember a thing. The only part of *The Dance of Darkness* I remember is the darkness part."

THE
SHAMPOOED
POOCH

"Cousin Will! What a surprise!" Mrs Trifle said, opening the front door to her posh cousin Wilhemina. "Is it that day again? It seems like it was only last month that you were here. Where's your dog?"

It was the day of the Bogusville Canine Society's annual dog show and Cousin Wilhemina — who wouldn't normally be caught dead in a little bush town like Bogusville — had arrived to win all the top prizes as she always did.

"He's in the box," Cousin Wilhemina said, marching into the lounge room with a big wooden box that had the name FREDDINGTON painted on both sides in huge blue-and-gold letters. "No time to spare," she said, pushing Selby off the carpet with her foot and folding down the sides of the box. "If we're going to win again this year we've got to get to work."

Inside the box was every sort of brush and clipper and nail file, and bottles and bottles of coloured liquids. Cousin Wilhemina reached into a mass of hair curlers and hair driers and pulled out one small dog.

Selby watched as Cousin Wilhemina shampooed Freddie and then dyed his fur and set it in curlers.

"Excuse me, Cousin Will," Dr Trifle said, looking up from his newspaper and wondering why anyone in their right mind would want to dye a dog," but you've made Freddington blue."

"Lavender," Cousin Wilhemina said, correcting him. "Last year he was deep apricot. This year his show name is Freddington Lavender Lilyblush and he'll be lavender all over."

"A lavender poodle," Dr Trifle said thoughtfully. "What will they think of next?"

"These days you have to think of a gimmick if you want to win Best in Show, dear," Cousin Wilhemina said, drying Freddie with an electric hair drier and then brushing his long lavender coat till it shone like a neon light. "Gone are the days when you could enter an ordinary dog without a lot of preparation and expect to win anything at all except, of course, Best in Breed. Winning Best in Breed in a town like Bogusville," she said, making her lip curl slightly as she said it, "should be no problem. Most of the dogs will be at least half mongrel — no offence to your Selby. My beautiful Freddie will probably be the only pure anything in the whole show."

"Mongrel, schmongrel," Selby thought as he looked at Freddie's sad little eyes. "She doesn't treat him like a dog, she treats him like a stuffed toy. Poor little pup."

"He's in the peak of condition," Cousin Wilhemina said, clipping a little fur here and there, and then putting a garland of flowers around his neck. "He's a real champion, aren't you sweet-ums?"

"He looks like a barrister's wig with eyes," Selby thought. "The dog show judge won't know whether to give him a prize or pick him up and put him on his head."

Later, at the dog show, Selby and the Trifles waited next to Cousin Wilhemina as a crowd of dog owners took turns parading their dogs in front of the judge. But all eyes were on Cousin Wilhemina, waiting for a glimpse at Freddington Lavender Lilyblush, who was hidden in his box, to surprise them at the last minute.

When no one was looking, Selby poked his head in the hole in the front of the box and had a good look at Freddie.

"You poor thing," Selby thought. "You're not just a piece of fluff to be dragged around from one dog show to the next. You're a thinking, feeling dog like the rest of us. To Cousin Will you're nothing but a hairdo on a lead. But I have an idea!" Selby thought, jumping into the box and ripping the garland of flowers from Freddie's neck.

He grabbed a pair of clippers, flipped the little dog on his back and started shearing him as though he were shearing a sheep.

"Okay, Fred," Selby said, leaving a patch of hair here and a patch of hair there so Freddie wouldn't win a prize for the best Mexican Hairless by accident, "we're going to show Cousin Will that there's a real dog under that fur."

Selby took some bottles of dye and coloured the tufts of fur red, green, brown and strawberry pink, as Freddie wagged his tail furiously. And to finish the job he reached outside the box and picked up some crushed paper cups and other pieces of litter, put them on a string and hung them around Freddie's neck.

"There you go, Freddie," Selby muttered as he hopped out of the box just in time to hear the judge call Freddie's name. "A garland of garbage, the perfect touch. Now you're my kind of dog."

"Come along, Freddington," Cousin Wilhemina said, stepping out into the spotlight and expecting Freddie to follow two steps behind as he'd been trained to do, "we're on."

There was a sudden hush from the crowd and even the dogs stopped barking for a minute as Freddie leaped out of the box and began prancing around the ring. But the hush turned into a roar of laughter and cheering.

"Good grief!" Cousin Wilhemina shrieked, not quite loud enough for anyone to hear above the noise. "Someone's plucked my pooch! I'll scalp the scoundrel!"

Then suddenly the judge's open mouth clamped shut and a smile crossed his lips. "Amazing!" he cried, looking at Freddie and thinking how his teenage son and daughter looked when they went to the Smash and Grab Video Parlour on Friday nights. "A punk dog! Brilliant! Whoever would have thought of it! I'm going to award Freddington not only Best in Breed and Best in Show but Best New Look Dog of the Show!"

With this, there was a cheer of approval and Cousin Wilhemina began to smile in spite of herself.

"I knew he'd win," she said to Dr and Mrs Trifle. "Freddie's a champion and no one can stop a champion. His next show name will be Fred Frenzy."

Selby just looked at the smiling Freddie.

"She's right," he thought, "you just can't keep a good dog down."

RAID ON PLANET KAPON

"Oh, wow!" Selby said, reading the entertainment page of the *Bogusville Banner* and seeing that the movie *Raid on Planet Kapon* had finally come to the Bogusville Bijou. "I've got to see it! I'll wait till Dr and Mrs Trifle are asleep and sneak out to the late show."

Selby waited outside the theatre till the movie was about to begin and then crept in in the dark and found a seat in the back row where no one would notice him. In a minute the film started with a roll of drums and some *ping ping ping ping zip* noises and then a crash of cymbals. Across the screen in a great burst of swirling galaxies and exploding stars came the title of the movie:

REVOLT OF THE UNIVERSE

Episode Eight

RAID ON PLANET KAPON

"Fantabulous!" Selby said, hanging his paws over the empty seat in front of him. "I've seen all the other movies in the series and this one is supposed to be the best of all of them!"

Then a lot of words came up on the screen, getting bigger as they went, and a deep voice read them out at the same time:

Prince Zak and Princess Su have made their way to Planet Kapon to live in peace after the end of the Third Galactic War. They have the all-powerful Star Web which was given to them by the Mighty Master of the Universe before he died. With the Star Web safely in the hands of the prince and princess the Universe will remain good and nice and its people will be able to do as they please forever. But little do they know, Lord Dar Coarse is gathering together the Forces of the Darkened Light to raid Planet Kapon and steal the Star Web.

"Crikey!" Selby said as another star exploded on the screen. "I thought Lord Dar Coarse was killed when he fell screaming into the sun at the end of the last movie."

"The time has come to crush Prince Zak and Princess Su," Lord Dar Coarse said to his evil robot Yor Wun 2. "I don't want any accidents this time. Do you hear? No accidents! Let's get going."

Lord Dar Coarse and his fleet of hundreds of star ships sped through time and space till they reached Planet Kapon. Then, hovering in the darkness above the tiny planet, Lord Dar Coarse pressed a button that said FORCE FIELD and suddenly all the lights in the houses on Planet Kapon went off, including the nightlight in the bubble house where Prince Zak and Princess Su lay sleeping.

Lord Dar Coarse's star ship drifted silently down to the surface of the planet while the other ships stayed behind.

"Wake up!" Selby said, almost loud enough to be heard above the music. "They're coming to get the Web!"

Lord Dar Coarse and Yor Wun 2 got out of their ship and stood for a moment in the darkness outside the prince and princess's house. The villains took out their light sabres and were ready to burst in through the door when suddenly the prince and princess appeared on the top of the bubble above them.

"The force of right! The freedom of might!" Prince Zak yelled (as he always did), and he threw the Star Web — which looked to Selby like the net that Phil Philpot put over his peach tree to keep the birds from eating his peaches, only the Star Web glittered with blue light — over Lord Dar Coarse and Yor Wun 2.

"Great stuff!" Selby said, climbing right up onto the back of the seat to get a better view. "This is so exciting! This is wonderful!"

Just when the prince and princess were escaping from the planet with the Star Web, the movie suddenly stopped and the theatre went completely black except for the manager's torch.

"Ladies and gentlemen," the manager said, "I regret to say that the power has gone off all over Bogusville. You may wait for a while and see if it comes on again and we can finish the movie, or come to the box office and I'll give you your money back. I'm sorry for the inconvenience."

"What a disappointment," Selby thought as he shot past the ticket office without stopping to get back the money which he hadn't paid anyway. "I'd better go home. It could be hours till the power comes back on."

Selby was on his way through the middle of Bogusville when he noticed two dark figures standing in the road. They both held torches with long red cones on their ends.

"I don't want any accidents this time," one of the men said in a low voice. "Let's get going."

"Crikey!" Selby said, stopping dead in his tracks. "That's what Lord Dar Coarse said to Yor Wun 2! Oh, no! Look at the light sabres! It's them! They've shut off the power with their force field! I'd better tell the police."

Selby tore back to the police station to find Constable Long and Sergeant Short, but the building was empty.

"They've captured the cops already!" Selby said. "I'll have to take matters into my own paws."

Selby raced to Phil Philpot's house and pulled the net off the peach tree.

"I don't have the Star Web so this will have

94

to do," he said as he ran back to the spot where the two men stood in the road.

Then, holding the net in his mouth, Selby crept up a tree and walked quietly out on a limb that hung over the men.

Suddenly Selby yelled out in plain English: "The forces of right! The freedom of might!" only it sounded more like: "The gorses of gright! The greedom of gite!" with his mouth full of net — and with this he dropped the net down over the two men and jumped after it.

"I've got you now, Lord Dar Coarse," Selby said, winding the net around the two struggling men. "And as for your evil robot, you can kiss him goodbye. He'll be nothing but nuts and bolts when I'm finished."

"Hey! Who is that?" the men yelled. "What's going on?"

Just then the lights of Bogusville went back on, revealing Constable Long and Sergeant short tangled in the net with their traffic torches still glowing. Selby looked at the policemen and backed slowly away thinking of a thousand places he'd rather be at the moment.

"Hey!" yelled Sergeant Short, looking right at Selby. "Isn't that Mayor Trifle's dog?"

"Why yes it is," Constable Long said, pulling the net off them. "He must have been right here when this happened. He probably saw the person who did it."

"Yeah," said Sergeant Short. "If only dogs could talk, I think someone would have some serious explaining to do."

"Gulp," Selby thought as he dashed back to the Bijou to see the rest of *Raid on Planet Kapon.* "If the lights had come on two seconds sooner, *I'd* be the one doing the serious explaining."

SELBY DELIVERS THE GOODS

Selby was in a panic. It all started when Mrs Trifle phoned for takeaway food from the Trifles' favourite restaurant, The Spicy Onion. Whenever Mrs Trifle ordered food from The Spicy Onion she got a special dish of prawns cooked in peanut sauce just for Selby. Always — except this time. Selby had walked into the room while Mrs Trifle was on the phone and heard her say: "Yes, that's right, the beef thing-a-me and the egg plant whatsit and the zucchini alla what's-her-name — I'm terrible at those foreign names — yes, that's the whole order. Thank you."

"*No peanut prawns!*" Selby thought as his stomach rumbled with hunger at the idea of them. "What have I done wrong? How can they expect me to survive on a diet of Chunk-O-Gravy Hunks and Dry-Mouth Dog Biscuits. I'm a thinking, feeling dog and I need some variety in my diet. Crumbs, you don't suppose she … hates me? No. She's such a wonderful person. She couldn't hate anyone, not even me. I'm sure she just forgot to order the prawns. I'll fix it up."

Selby waited till Mrs Trifle had left the study and gently nudged the door closed. He picked up the phone and dialled The Spicy Onion.

"This is Dr Trifle of Bunya-Bunya Crescent," Selby said, putting on his best imitation of the doctor's voice. "I'd just like to add a dish of peanut prawns to the order my wife phoned in earlier."

"Yes sir, of course," Phil Philpot, the owner and cook of The Spicy Onion said. "Is that all?"

"That's all," Selby said. "When do you think you'll be bringing it around to my house?"

"You want it delivered to your house?" Phil Philpot asked, sounding a bit surprised and a little irritable after all the questioning from the police who had just returned the net from his peach tree.

"Of course," Selby said, wondering what better place to send the Trifles' dinner than to the Trifles' house.

"Okay," Phil Philpot said. "It'll be there in half an hour."

"Thanks," Selby said, quietly putting down the phone as the Trifles' footsteps approached.

"Are you ready to go now, dear?" Mrs Trifle asked her husband.

"Yes, almost ready," the doctor answered. "I just have to find the theatre tickets."

"To go? Theatre tickets?" Selby wondered as he lay on the carpet watching. "Aren't they going to eat first?"

Dr Trifle looked through every drawer of the desk twice and then went back for a third look.

"By the way," he said to Mrs Trifle, "have you organised dinner for the bushfire brigade?"

"I rang The Spicy Onion," said Mrs Trifle. "It's going to be delivered to the fire brigade hall. It's all taken care of."

A shiver shot up Selby's spine.

"Cripes," he thought. "The food wasn't for us after all! What have I done? I'd better phone The

Spicy Onion straight away before they deliver the food here instead of the fire brigade hall."

For the next twenty minutes Selby watched the phone anxiously but Dr Trifle continued to search his desk for the theatre tickets.

"Oh, here they are," Dr Trifle said, pulling them out of the book he was reading, *The Inventor's Guide to Fast-Moving Cam Shafts and Water-Driven Floral Clocks*, where he'd been using them for a bookmark. "We'd better get going or we'll be late."

After the Trifles drove out of the driveway, Selby dashed for the phone only to hear a knock at the door. He peeked out the front window and saw Phil Philpot driving away. When he opened the door he found twenty-one boxes of hot food — plus one box of peanut prawns.

"Crumbs," Selby said, dashing to the phone only to find that The Spicy Onion was closed for the night. "I'll have to get the food to the bushfire brigade hall myself — quick!"

So Selby was in a panic. He had a problem: how was he to carry all those boxes of food all the way across Bogusville?

"I know!" he said, remembering the old tea trolley that Dr Trifle had left out to be taken to the tip. "I'll just put it all on the trolley and push it there."

It was dark and no one saw Selby pushing the loaded trolley along the footpath that led up Mulga Hill towards the bushfire brigade hall. And if pushing it uphill was hard, holding it back going down the hill was even harder.

"But what am I doing?" Selby suddenly thought, jumping on the trolley. "I'll just ride it down the hill and I'll be there in no time."

The trolley took off like a runaway bowling ball, jumping the kerb and tearing down the middle of the street with Selby hanging onto it, and the food, for dear life.

"Oh, no!" Selby said, looking ahead to the bushfire brigade hall with its front door open and all the fire fighters sitting at a long table having their meeting. "I've got to slow this thing down."

Selby put his hind paws on the ground and dragged them but the trolley only went faster and faster towards the open door.

"This is serious!" Selby thought, trying to stay cool but not succeeding. "This is more than serious — it's a disaster! Even if I can stop this thing I'm a done dog. They'll see me. Everyone will know that it was me who phoned The Spicy Onion. Then they'll know that I can talk! This isn't a disaster, it's a catastrophe! I've got to think of something fast!"

The hall came closer and closer and Selby suddenly realised that he was about to run down all the fire fighters in Bogusville at one go.

"I've got to warn them," he thought. "What can you say to clear a hall full of fire fighters fast? I've got it!"

"*Fire! Fire! Fire!*" he screamed.

The second they heard the word *fire!* the fire fighters ran for every door and window in the hall and they didn't stop till they were sitting safely in Bogusville Creek.

Meanwhile, Selby tore through the empty hall, throwing all the boxes of food onto the long table as he went, and then shot out the back door and straight into a thicket of lantana.

In a few minutes the fire fighters returned, dripping wet, to the hall.

"I didn't see any fire," one of them said.

"Neither did I," said another. "I didn't even smell smoke. But look! Phil Philpot's been in and brought us our dinner. He must have been in and out of here in a flash. That must be the fastest delivery on record."

That night when the Trifles arrived home they were careful not to wake Selby who was sleeping on the carpet.

"Very strange," Dr Trifle said. "He's all scratched. Do you suppose he's been in a fight?"

"Who, Selby?" said Mrs Trifle. "Selby doesn't fight. He's too smart for that. Whatever happened it must have made him happy. Just look at that smile on his face. I haven't seen him looking so happy since the last time he had takeaway food from The Spicy Onion."

"Hmmmmm ...," Dr Trifle hmmmmmed thoughtfully, "that's funny. I could swear I smell peanut prawns."

SELBY'S BEAUTIFUL BODY

"What *are* you doing with that bicycle?" Mrs Trifle asked Dr Trifle as she bounded out of the bedroom in her new tracksuit. "No tinkering, now. It's exercise time."

"I'm not tinkering, dear," Dr Trifle said, removing the brakes from the bicycle he was working on in the lounge room. "I'm going to turn this old thing into an exerciser. I'll make a stand for it so that the back wheel is off the ground. Then I can sit right here and read a book or watch TV and still get plenty of exercise."

"What a marvellous idea — but you'd better stop now, *Slim-Slam* is on," Mrs Trifle said, turning on the television to their favourite TV exercise program, *Slim-Slam*, and watching as Ronald Ringlets and the Slim-Slam Dancers bounced out on stage, pumping their fists in the air to a pop tune.

"A one and a two and a one and a two," Ronald sang, "love your body and your body loves you."

Dr Trifle dropped his spanner and he and Mrs Trifle joined in as Ronald Ringlets and the Slim-Slam Dancers began running on the spot. The pounding on the floor woke Selby.

"I don't think I've ever been so fit," Dr Trifle said as the sweat poured from his forehead.

"Neither have I," Mrs Trifle said. "Three days and I'm sure we've both lost kilos already. Another week and we'll have to stand twice in the same spot just to cast a shadow, as my father used to say."

"A one and a two and a one two three!" Ronald Ringlets yelled, pumping his knees up to his chest. "You love you and I love me!"

"The (*puff*) other (*puff*) thing," Mrs Trifle said, lifting her knees higher and higher, "is that exercise is supposed to give you energy. If I can get in shape I won't need to take a holiday."

"I've got an idea!" Dr Trifle said, suddenly turning off the TV set. "Let's go for a real jog around Bogusville and get some fresh air and sunshine."

"Exercise," Selby muttered as soon as the Trifles were safely out of the house. "What a waste of time. They're such wonderful people just the way they are. Why don't they sit back quietly and enjoy life the way I do? They could read books or newspapers," Selby said, suddenly remembering something. "Come to think of it, I missed the last episode of my favourite comic strip, *Wonderful Wanda, Maker of Music*. I wonder what happened to the latest copy of the *Bogusville Banner*. It must be with the old newspapers in the garden shed."

Selby went out the back door and across the lawn to the shed.

"Hmmmmmmm," he hmmmmmmmed as he looked at the lock on the door. "I'll have to squeeze through the hole in the back where the broken boards are."

"Ooooooomph!" he said, getting stuck halfway through. "Either this hole is smaller or — no! It can't be! I don't believe it! I've been eating the same amounts of the same old food — except for one order of peanut prawns from The Spicy Onion — how could I have put on weight?"

Selby struggled to get through the hole, but it was hopeless. Finally he pulled himself back and lay panting on the grass.

"This is a disaster! What will I do? The old newspapers will be collected on Thursday. I'll miss *Wonderful Wanda!*"

Selby ran back to the house and turned on the TV. Ronald Ringlets was slicing the air with his arms and touching his toes.

"This is just what all you Slim-Slammers need to keep your tum tums trim," he squealed. "A one and a two and a one and a two."

"If Mrs Trifle can lose kilos in a few days at the speed she goes," Selby said, standing on his hind feet and swooping down touching paw to paw, "I'll go at double speed and, by Wednesday,

I'll be slipping in and out of the garden shed like a ferret after rabbits."

"And now the Slim-Slam shuffle!" Ronald Ringlets screamed, and his curly hair bounced up and down like a hundred springs. "Put your hands on your hips and shuffle your shoes around the carpet. Bend your whole body while you do it. To the music now," he sang. "Let's do that slip-slap hip-happy Slim-Slam shoeshine shuffle! And a one and a one and a one two three, I can see you but you can't see me!"

"This had better work," Selby said, shuffling along at lightning speed and then throwing open the door to get some fresh air, "because it's (puff puff) painful!"

"All right all you beautiful Slim-Slam slimmers!" Ronald Ringlets yelled as he jumped on his exerciser bicycle. "If you want to take pounds off your paunch and years off your age, just remember: one two three five six four, pedal that bike now, more more more!"

Selby grabbed Dr Trifle's exerciser bicycle and propped up the back of it with two stacks of books to keep the back wheel off the ground. He jumped on it and started pedalling furiously.

"I may be a little out of shape," he said, trying to keep up with Ronald Ringlets, "but an out-of-shape dog can beat an in-shape human any day of the week."

Selby pedalled faster and faster till the back wheel made a whooshing sound as it sped through the air. Then, suddenly, the bicycle lurched and fell off the books and when the speeding wheel hit the carpet, Selby and the bike shot out the open door and down Bunya-Bunya Crescent.

"Cripes!" Selby yelled when he realised that there were no brakes and that he was headed straight down the steepest part of Mulga Hill towards town. "I think I remember doing this before! Somebody save me!"

Selby went faster and faster till — when he passed the exhausted Trifles who were puffing their way up the hill — he was nothing more than a brown streak.

"That's funny," Dr Trifle said, slowing down to a walk. "Did you feel that breeze?"

"Yes," Mrs Trifle said, wiping her brow and sitting down by the side of the road. "And did you hear it?"

"Hear it, dear?"

"Why, yes. It made a sound that sounded curiously like someone saying 'Heeeeeeeeeelp!'."

"Yooooooowwwwwwwweeeel," Selby screamed, barely making the corner at the bottom of the hill and then tearing out of control through two of the longest flowerbeds in the Bogusville Memorial Rose Garden.

Later, Selby sneaked back into the Trifle house with the bicycle just ahead of the Trifles. The three of them lay back on the lounge-room floor watching *The Lucky Millions Quiz Quest*.

"I don't know if all this puffing and panting is worth it," Dr Trifle said, barely able to keep his eyes open. "I'm so tired all the time I can't get anything done. Yesterday I started filling in the hole in the back of the garden shed and now I don't know when I'll have the energy to finish the job."

"I know what you mean," Mrs Trifle said. "Somehow it's no substitute for a good holiday. I only wish we had the money to get away from Bogusville for a while. But just a minute," she said suddenly, "don't fix that hole in the shed.

Put it back the way it was. Selby likes to go in there for a snooze."

"Crumbs, the hole *was* getting smaller after all. And I thought I was getting fat," Selby thought as he pulled another rose thorn out of his leg. "But I'll say one thing for Ronald Ringlets and his Slim-Slammers, he said that exercise would take years off my age and he was nearly right. I almost lost all my years at once!"

LUCKY MILLIONS

"Poor Mrs Trifle," Selby thought as he lay alone in the house curled up in the bean bag watching *The Lucky Millions Quiz Quest*. "It really isn't fair. She works so hard. If only I could earn a lot of money and give it to her. Then she could have a proper holiday."

No sooner were these words out of his mouth than Larry Limelight, the compere of *The Lucky Millions Quiz Quest* said something that made Selby leap to his feet: "And now," Larry screamed, flashing a set of teeth that looked like the keys of a concert grand piano, "we have a super-duper special for all you folks at home. This new feature is called the Special

113

Viewers' Phone-in Holiday History Question. The first person to phone in the correct answer to this question will win a holiday for two on a yacht on the Barrier Reef. Listen carefully now," Larry said, lowering his voice nearly to a whisper. "The question is: what country did Napoleon crown himself king of in 1804?"

"I know it! I know it!" Selby yelled as he ran to the phone and dialled *Lucky Millions*, thinking all the while about the TV program he had seen three weeks before called *Napoleon: the Long and the Short of Him*.

Selby listened as the phone rang and he watched Larry Limelight on TV picking up the receiver.

"The answer," Selby said coolly before Larry Limelight could open his mouth, "is ... nothing."

Selby watched the compere's smile fade.

"I'm terribly sorry," the man said, "your answer is incorrect. But thank you for being a sport. We'd like to send you a special *Lucky Millions* T-shirt——"

"Hold your T-shirt, Larry," Selby said. "Napoleon didn't become king of anything in 1804. He became *emperor* of France in 1804 and king of Italy in 1805."

Larry Limelight read the card in his hand and flashed a blinding smile.

"Yes!" he screamed. "You've got it! You've just won a glorious trip for two to the fabulous Barrier Reef on the yacht of your dreams. Now could I please have your name?"

"Name (gulp) ... ah, er ... let's see now," Selby said.

"We have to have your name to send you the tickets," Larry Limelight said with a laugh.

"Well . . . of course," Selby said. "This is Dr Trifle of number five Bunya-Bunya Crescent, Bogusville."

"Way out there in Bogusville!" the compere said. "That's great!"

"Yes, and while you're about it, could you please include my dog on these tickets. Mrs Trifle and I never travel without our dog," Selby said, adding, "he's a wonderful dog and we just wouldn't know what to do —"

"No worries," Larry Limelight said, putting the phone down. "The man never travels without his dog. Isn't that great? Now let's get on with the show!"

"I did it!" Selby screamed as he danced around the room. "I blinkin' well did it!" and then he started singing the *Lucky Millions* theme song:

"Love that money madness.
See those dollars drifting down.
Sing away your troubles,
Hang upside down."

The next day Selby looked out the front window in time to see a man with the *Lucky*

Millions crest on his blazer tramp through a bed of petunias on the way to the house.

"Uh-oh, what's this?" Selby said, feeling lucky that Mrs Trifle was out at a council meeting and Dr Trifle was at the Bogusville Memorial Rose Garden working on the floral clock. "Why is he coming here? I thought they were going to *send* the tickets."

"Dr Trifle!" the man called out, pounding his fist on the front door. "Open up! I have your holiday tickets."

"Slide them under the door," Selby called back.

"You can't have the tickets till you sign the form."

"What form?" Selby asked. "Nobody said anything about a form."

"It's the one that says that *Lucky Millions* isn't responsible if the yacht sinks and you drown. Just a formality, of course. Now open up please, I've got to get back to the city."

"I can't open the door," Selby said, searching the corners of his brain for reasons why he couldn't open the door.

"Why not?"

"The house is under quarantine," Selby said, putting on a raspy voice. "I have (mumble mumble) fever and no one's allowed to come near me."

"What kind of fever?" the man asked.

"I have," Selby shouted and then he let his voice drop again and he put a paw over his mouth, "(mumble mumble) fever."

"I still can't hear you. It sounds like *mumble mumble* fever."

"It's doodlyboop fever," Selby said, "and it's very catching."

"I've never heard of doodlyboop fever."

"Most people who hear of it are dead by dinnertime," Selby said. "Just push the blinkin' paper under the door and I'll sign it."

"I can't get it under," the man said, crumpling the paper as he tried. "There's not enough room."

"Okay. I'll open the door and go into my study. Just give the paper to my dog and he'll bring it to me," Selby said. "But I warn you, don't set foot in the house if you know what's good for you."

Selby unlocked the door and let the breeze blow it slowly open.

"Here you go, mutt," the man said, thrusting the paper into Selby's mouth and giving him a good slap on the behind as he turned to go. "Get that stupid man to sign the thing. I've got to get cracking. It's a long way back to civilisation."

Selby dashed into the darkened study, hopped on the chair and turned on the desk lamp to read the small print on the form.

"Mutt, schmutt," Selby said, angry at the slap on the behind and at the man calling Dr Trifle stupid. "Well the form seems all right. I'll just sign it and get rid of him."

Selby signed the paper using his best imitation of the doctor's handwriting. He had folded it and put it in his mouth when suddenly the shadow of the *Lucky Millions* man fell across the desk.

"Hey!" the man said. "What's going on here? Where's Dr Trifle?"

Selby turned his head slowly and looked at the man.

"In a second," he thought, "he'll know that Dr Trifle isn't here. In another second he'll know the horrible truth: that I'm the only reading, writing and talking dog in all of Australia and — as far as I know — in the world. This could be my last second of freedom. I've got to act fast."

The man snatched the paper from Selby's mouth just as Selby's paw hit the button on the desk lamp and cast the room into darkness. Before the man's eyes could adjust to the dark, Selby yelled, "Get out of here, you fool! Get out before my dog rips you to pieces!"

Selby growled and sank his teeth into the man's leg as he ran out of the study and straight out the front door and through the petunias.

"Help! Call off your dog!" the man cried as he leaped into his car, throwing the envelope with the tickets in it out the window as he sped away.

"Silly man," Selby said, spitting out a piece of pants and picking up the envelope. "Why do people insist on making life so difficult?"

A BUSMAN'S HOLIDAY

"This is all very odd," Dr Trifle said to Mrs Trifle as they stood on the pier waiting for the yacht to come and take them out to the Barrier Reef. "I still don't see how we won these tickets."

"I told you. It was just luck," Mrs Trifle said, feeling a little tired after the long flight from Bogusville. "I found a note in the letterbox with the tickets telling us all about it. Apparently they picked our names out of a hat. The point is," she said, patting the smiling Selby, "when you need things, somehow they happen. We both needed a holiday and here we are."

"My heavens," Dr Trifle said, watching as a beat-up boat pulled into the pier. "What a

121

funny-looking old thing that is. I wonder when our dream yacht will be along."

"At your command," the captain said, jumping ashore and saluting Mrs Trifle as she tried to shake his hand. "This is the *Golden Doldrum* and I'm your driver, Slick Slipway."

"But … but …" said Dr Trifle, wondering why the deck was filled with rows of seats just like a city bus, "we're waiting for the yacht of our dreams. Surely this can't be it. This is rather more like a … er … nightmare, if you don't mind my saying so."

"If you're the people who won *The Lucky Millions Quiz Quest Magic Dream Cruise* then I'm your man and this is your yacht," Captain Slipway said, shaking the hand of Dr Trifle who, in his confusion, was trying to salute.

"But where are the other passengers?" Mrs Trifle asked. "And where's the crew?"

"There aren't any, and you're looking at him," Captain Slipway said, answering both questions in one sentence and polishing the metal part on the front of his cap — which wasn't a captain's hat but the one he used to wear when he drove the 275 bus. "Now hop on

122

and move to the rear of the boat. Next stop Nothing Lagoon," he added as Selby jumped aboard.

"All right," Dr Trifle said. "You *are* going to take us to the Dolphin Research Station on Dolphin Island, I trust. My old friend Dr Septimus C. Squirt is expecting us."

"All in good time," said Slick. "My instructions are to take you to Nothing Lagoon first. That's the route and there'll be no arguments. Leave the brain work to me. Just sit back and have a rest."

Nothing Lagoon was a pond in the middle of a tiny island shaped like a doughnut with a bite out of it. The island was called Nothing Atoll. Captain Slipway steered the *Golden Doldrum* into the middle of the lagoon and turned around and started out.

"Hold on, just a minute," Mrs Trifle said.

"Aren't we going to dock?"

"You mean stop?" Slick said, making no attempt to do so. "I'm sorry. You didn't pull the cord so we didn't stop. Those are the rules," he said, pointing to a long list of rules that hung from the back of his driver's seat.

"You mean we're just going to sail in and sail out?" Dr Trifle asked.

"I'm just the driver. I don't make the rules," said Slick. "Next stop Pipe Dream Island. Next stop, that is, if you remember to pull the cord."

No sooner were they away from Nothing Atoll than the engine of the *Golden Doldrum* suddenly gave out and wouldn't start again.

"What do we do now?" asked Dr Trifle who was feeling slightly seasick as well as angry.

"We rig the sails," said Slick.

"Who, exactly, is *we*?" asked Mrs Trifle.

"Well it's not me," said the captain, trying once again to start the engine.

"Well it's not us either," Dr Trifle said. "We're the passengers. We don't work."

"I'm the driver. I don't work either," Slick said, remembering how easy it used to be when the 275 bus broke down and he called the depot for another bus. "Now hop to it, we're falling behind schedule."

For the next three hours Dr and Mrs Trifle dashed about hauling halyards and lacing lanyards while Captain Slipway called out orders and the *Golden Doldrum* sailed towards Pipe Dream Island.

"If that old sea-dog yells at me one more time," Dr Trifle said to Mrs Trifle, wondering whether it had been good luck or bad luck to win the Magic Dream Cruise (and not knowing that it was neither), "we'll just have to tell him to turn around and take us back to port."

"Sea-dog, schmee-dog," muttered Selby as he crawled under a copy of the *Bogusville Banner* and secretly read the weather report. "Hmmmmmmmm. If this weather map means what I think it does we're in for a storm any minute now."

"Pull that rope!" Slick yelled, having a very good time of it now. "Bring that wooden thing around to the other side and don't hang so far over the front!"

Just then the storm hit and Dr and Mrs Trifle — who were hanging over the bow — were knocked into the water at the same instant that Slick's glasses were knocked onto the deck.

"Stop! Help!" the Trifles yelled as the boat sailed past. "Throw us a line — I mean, a rope!"

"I'm sorry," Captain Slipway called back, seeing four blurry people waving in the waves where there should have been only two, and not recognising any of them. "The next bus will be along in a few minutes. We're full-up. Now where did those glasses go?" he added, feeling around on the deck.

Selby watched as the Trifles drifted into the distance, knowing that Slick wouldn't be able to sail the *Golden Doldrum* back to them all by himself even if he could find his glasses.

"This whole disaster is my fault," he thought. "I never should have answered the Special

Viewers' Phone-in Holiday History Question. I only wanted to send these dear, sweet people on a holiday and now look what I've done. I've got to do something quick even if it means giving away my (gulp) secret."

Selby walked up to Slick and stood on his hind legs with his paws on his hips.

"All right, Slick," he announced. "This is an emergency and I'm taking over. Your passengers have fallen overboard and you and I are going to sail back — I mean, drive back — and save them. You just hold tight to the steering wheel till we're ready to come about — I mean, turn around."

"Twin talking dogs," Slick said, holding tight to the wheel. "They must be on the wrong bus."

Selby rushed around the deck pulling pulleys and shortening sheets.

"Hard to starboard! Ready to come about!" Selby yelled at the bewildered captain. "I mean, make a U-turn!"

Slick stuck out his arm and signalled a right turn and soon was sailing back towards the Trifles with Selby yelling, "A little to the right!" and "More to the left!"

In a few minutes, Dr and Mrs Trifle were climbing on board.

"Thank goodness you've saved us," Mrs Trifle said, wiping her face with a towel. "I was afraid you were going to sail off without us."

"Don't thank me," Slick said. "Thank those two talking dogs over there."

Dr Trifle looked around at Selby who was lying on the *Bogusville Banner* reading the latest episode of *Wonderful Wanda*.

"Two talking dogs, was it?" Mrs Trifle said, picking up Slick Slipway's glasses and handing them to him. "Put these on and maybe you'll see them more clearly. Now let's get going. Dr Squirt is waiting for us."

"Just as well they had an old sea-dog like me around," Selby thought.

SELBY SINKS
TO NEW DEPTHS

The *Golden Doldrum* docked at Dolphin Island and Dr Septimus C. Squirt, the director of the Dolphin Research Station, was there to meet the Trifles.

"Blinky!" Dr Squirt said, clapping Dr Trifle so hard on the back that he nearly fell into the water. "How good to see you and Mrs Trifle. I can't wait to show you all the exciting work we're doing here. Come along, there's no time to waste."

Selby and the Trifles followed Dr Squirt to a large building where the director had an office packed with every sort of electronic device. There he could sit and look through a window into a huge tank and study a dolphin.

Selby put his nose up to the glass and in an instant the dolphin swam down and put his nose on the other side, giving Selby a start.

"I'm on the brink of a great discovery," Dr Squirt said, twiddling the dials of his instruments. "Soon I will be able to talk to animals."

"What makes him think that animals want to talk to him?" Selby thought, feeling a bit sorry for the dolphin.

"We captured Dizzy only three weeks ago," Dr Squirt went on, "and already he's said, '*bleep beek gleep squeak*'."

"He said what?" Mrs Trifle said, wondering why Dr Squirt would want to talk to a dolphin and what he would say if he could.

"'*Bleep beek gleep squeak*'," Dr Squirt repeated. "Music to the ears, isn't it?"

"Not my sort of music," Selby thought as Dizzy tapped the glass in front of him with one flipper.

"And what does it mean?" Dr Trifle asked.

"I'm not quite sure," Dr Squirt said. "It could mean 'throw me a herring'. He seems to think about food quite a lot."

"It probably means 'stop staring at me, you silly scientific twit'," thought Selby, who was glad he'd never said "*bleep beek gleep squeak*" — or anything else, for that matter — to Dr Squirt.

Dizzy swam round and round the pool and then pressed his nose to the window and said, "*Squeak bleek beep beek*."

"Now I think that means, 'throw me a mackerel'," Dr Squirt said. "I haven't worked out all the finer points of the language but soon Dizzy and I will be having long and intimate conversations."

"At least you'll be able to tell each other when you're hungry," Selby thought.

Dr Squirt opened the door that led to the top part of the pool and went upstairs. He pulled a mackerel out of a plastic bucket and held it over the water. Dizzy made a tight circle and then leaped up out of the water and grabbed it out of Dr Squirt's hand.

"Raw fish," Selby thought, remembering that he hadn't eaten all day, and also remembering his favourite TV cooking show which had told him how the Japanese sometimes eat raw fish. "I think I could go for a munch of mackerel right now."

"For the rest of the tour," Dr Squirt said, returning to his office, "we'll have to leave your little dog behind. There are ladders where we're going, I don't think he could manage them."

No sooner were they out of sight than the thought of raw fish got the best of Selby and he opened the door and dashed upstairs to the top of the pool.

"Sorry Dizzy," he thought, plunging his head into the fish bucket and pulling out a mackerel, "but we've all got to eat."

Dizzy, misunderstanding Selby's intention and thinking it was feeding time again, swam in a circle and then leaped into the air, grabbing the fish's tail in his teeth. All of which would have been okay except that Selby, who had just decided that raw fish tasted horrible and that he wasn't going to eat it, didn't let go fast enough and soon he was flying through the air and into the middle of the pool. All of which still would have been okay if Selby hadn't been the only dog in Australia and — for all he knew — the world that couldn't swim.

Selby thrashed about on the surface of the water and suddenly his life flashed before his eyes: he saw himself sitting in front of the TV watching Basil the butler. He remembered the exact moment when he realised that he could understand people-talk. He remembered teaching himself to speak and he remembered deciding that he was going to keep his talking a deep, dark secret — even if it killed him.

"Deep? Dark?" Selby thought, suddenly sinking under the surface and then bobbing up again. *"Even if it killed me?"* he thought again, suddenly thinking that dying would be going too far and yelling out at the top of his voice, "Help me! Save me! Get me out of this stupid pool! I can talk! I admit I can talk! I'll tell you everything you want to know, just get me out of here!"

Just then Dizzy picked up Selby with his nose and raced up and down, throwing and catching him like a beach ball.

"*Squeak bleep*," Dizzy squealed, throwing Selby out of the pool and watching him race down the stairs through the doorway and into Dr Squirt's office.

"Crumbs!" Selby thought, shaking the water out of his fur, and thinking how happy he was to be alive — but wishing he'd kept his mouth shut. "I hope Dr Squirt didn't hear me."

Just as Selby closed the door behind him and curled up innocently on the floor, Dr Squirt burst in with the Trifles close behind.

"What's happening?" Dr Squirt asked. "What was all that noise?"

"It sounded like ... like a voice," Dr Trifle said. "I could have sworn it was someone calling."

"Fortunately I always leave the tape recorder

going when I'm out of the office. I can just play it all back."

"Gulp," Selby thought, looking less and less innocent as he heard his cries for help on the tape recorder. "I'm a done dog this time. The evidence is right on the tape. There will be no denying it. I'll have to own up."

"He talked!" Dr Squirt yelled. "He spoke in the honest to goodness Queen's own English! An animal spoke! Oh joy of joys! I knew it would happen one day! And he said he'd tell us everything if we just let him out of the tank! Quick! Help me open the gate!"

"The silly nit thinks it was Dizzy calling for help," Selby thought, breathing a sigh of relief.

Dr Squirt and Mrs Trifle grabbed the valve and turned it and Dizzy shot out of the pool and into the ocean. They all dashed to the water's edge in time to see Dizzy swimming away.

"Stop!" Dr Squirt yelled after him. "You promised you'd tell me everything you know if I let you out! I upheld my end of the bargain, now it's your turn! Come back!" he called.

Dizzy jumped into the air and called back, "*Gleep bleep squeak bleep*," and was gone.

"What do you suppose that means?" Mrs Trifle asked.

"I think he's wishing me good luck," Dr Squirt said, waving and blinking back a tear.

"I think he said, 'better luck next time'," Selby thought as he and the Trifles boarded the *Golden Doldrum* for their trip back to the mainland. "That'll teach Dr Squirt to mess with not-so-dumb animals."

BOGUSVILLE FOREVER

Cracker Night was not Selby's favourite night of the year. It was not even his second favourite or his third. In fact it came close to last on his list of favourite nights, not because all the people in Bogusville went to the Bogusville Oval to see the Monster Fireworks Display, which was put on by the Fireworks Committee, but because Mrs Trifle always took him along, too.

"Selby just can't wait to see all the pretty fireworks," Mrs Trifle said to Dr Trifle as she patted Selby on the head. "Why, last year he just lay on the ground and watched every one of them. You could just tell he loved it."

"Let's make sure we bring him along tonight," Dr Trifle said, working on his sketch of the new water-driven floral clock at the Rose Garden. "Now let's see," he said to himself. "Maybe we should build a rain-barrel to catch the water that will drive the clock. Hmmmmmmmmmmmm."

"Fireworks," Selby thought as he secretly read the latest episode of *Wonderful Wanda* in the *Bogusville Banner.* "All that fizzing and banging rattles my nerves. Why can't people just sit down and relax? Why do they have to scare themselves silly and call it a good time?"

Just then there was a knock at the door and Phil Philpot, the owner of The Spicy Onion and head of the Fireworks Committee, burst in.

"I've got it!" he yelled. "I've got it!"

"What is it?" asked Mrs Trifle, hoping it wasn't measles or whooping cough.

"All we need is your permission, Mrs Mayor, and Big Beryl will burst into brilliance."

"I think we've got enough fireworks for tonight," Mrs Trifle said, remembering that Big Beryl was Phil Philpot's super-duper rocket and also remembering that wherever it went up and wherever it came down it always started bushfires.

"No, no!" Phil screamed. "You don't understand. It will be wonderful this year! I've ironed out all the problems. Picture this: everyone's down at the park and we set off the usual fizzers and bangers. Suddenly, just when everyone thinks it's over, you push a button and there's a rumbling over on Mount Gumboot. The rumbling builds to a roar and then up comes Big Beryl, the size of a garden shed, streaking across the sky."

"Spare me," Selby thought, trying to concentrate on how his favourite comic strip character Wonderful Wanda was going to escape from an enormous tuba.

"And that's not all!" Phil shrieked, pulling at the hair on the sides of his head till he looked like a big bonbon. "As it roars into the sky it drops a shower of colour like a huge rainbow. Then, suddenly, BOOM! Tiny rockets shoot out and burst into the letter B —"

"What tiny rockets?" Mrs Trifle interrupted.

"There are little rockets in the big rocket. They shoot out of holes in the sides of the big rocket. When the little rockets explode they will make the letter B in the sky," Phil explained.

"Does that make sense?"

"Yes, very good," Dr Trifle said. "But why a B?"

"I'm getting to that," Phil said. "Don't rush me. After the B there's another boom and more little rockets shoot out and explode in the shape of an O. Then another boom, and a G. By the time Big Beryl has crossed the sky it will have spelled out BOGUSVILLE FOREVER! Isn't that great?"

"But will it set the bush on fire?" Mrs Trifle asked.

"Impossible," Phil said. "It will come out of a hole in the ground and when it finishes writing BOGUSVILLE FOREVER a parachute will open and the rocket will drift slowly down. Any fires in the rocket will go out before it touches the ground. It's foolproof."

"That's what you said last year," Mrs Trifle said.

"Last year it didn't have the parachute," Phil said, getting excited again and stamping about the room, nearly tripping over Selby. "I'll tell

140

you what. If anything goes wrong, this town will get the biggest apology it's ever seen."

"All right," Mrs Trifle said, wondering just what a big apology was. "You win. Go ahead with Big Beryl."

"Yaaaaaaahhhhooooooo!" Phil shrieked. "You won't regret this."

That evening when Dr and Mrs Trifle were about to leave for Bogusville Oval, Selby was nowhere to be seen. In fact he had crept out the back door and was just climbing under the fence in the Bogusville Memorial Rose Garden when the Trifles finally got in their car.

"This," Selby said, with his copy of the *Bogusville Banner* and a torch to read it by, "will be the quietest place in town."

Selby found a freshly dug hole and climbed in, making himself comfortable on top of a rounded metal object, thinking that it must be something to do with Dr Trifle's new water-tank and not knowing that it was Big Beryl and that Mrs Trifle had decided there was less danger of fire if the rocket went up from the Rose Gardens instead of Mount Gumboot.

"This is the life," Selby said, lying back to re-read *Wonderful Wanda* for the fourth time and looking up occasionally to see the coloured glow in the air over the Bogusville Oval where the fireworks were fizzing and banging.

Then suddenly the fizzing and banging stopped and in the ground under Selby there was a rumbling that built to a roar. In a second Big Beryl shot into the air in a hail of sparks with Selby clinging to it for dear life.

"Help!" he screamed. "Get me down! Help!"

The rocket soared higher and higher, making a wide arc over Bogusville Oval where everyone could see the rainbow of colour streaming from its back, but no one could see the screaming Selby in the blackness of the night sky.

"Help!" he screamed again. "Save me!"

Just then there was a boom and tiny rockets shot out of the sides of Big Beryl, narrowly missing Selby's dangling hind legs. The rockets exploded, making a huge letter B, and there was a gasp and then a cheer from the crowd below.

"Please save me!" Selby screamed, and more tiny rockets shot out and exploded into the letter O.

Selby grabbed Big Beryl's nose cone tighter, pulling his feet up out of the way every time the little rockets shot out of its sides.

"Yoooooowwwwwwwwwch!" Selby yelled as the rockets for the first E in FOREVER hit his legs and spun every which way making a G and an I in the sky instead of an E. "Ow! That hurt! Help!"

Selby pulled his feet up as the rockets continued with a V and then an E, and then again the rockets of the letter R hit his feet and when they finally burst they looked more like an M and an E than an R.

"Iiiiiiiii-yi-yi-yi-yi-oooooooooch!" Selby screamed as he tried to beat out the flames on his furry feet, and Big Beryl's parachute opened and he drifted down into Bogusville Reserve.

"Cripes!" Selby cried as he hit the ground and started beating his feet in the leaves. "My blinkin' feet are on fire!"

Selby streaked through the bushes, setting fire to everything as he went, and then jumped into the only wet spot in Bogusville Creek.

"Phil Philpot did it again," he said, watching as the bushfire brigade arrived and quickly put

out the fire. "If only he'd stay out of the fireworks business and stick to making peanut prawns, I might get a little peace around this town. But I'll have to say one thing for him," Selby said, looking up and reading the letters in the sky that were supposed to say BOGUSVILLE FOREVER but which now said BOGUSVILLE FORGIVE ME, "that's the biggest apology I've ever seen."

AFTER WOOD or
THE EPIC LOG

Dr Trifle finally got that huge log into the fireplace and now he and Mrs Trifle are sleeping soundly on the lounge. So now I can write another note.

I hope you liked these stories about me. Most of them are true but you know how writers are—they always make stories a bit better than they already are. So don't believe every word you read. Anyway, I forgive the author for not telling the truth all the time and I hope you will too.

One thing I told him to lie about is Bogusville. It's a real town in Australia but Bogusville isn't it's real name. I made it up so no one would find me. We also lied about Dr and Mrs Trifle's name. That would be a dead give-away if they ever saw this book. Oh, and one more thing. My name's not Selby. That would be a give-away too. My name could be Spence and I could live with the MacWilliams of Mudgee. Or I could be Patches and live with the Catalanos of Benalla. (I'm not telling.) Of course I could be your dog. So go ahead and say, "I know it's you, Selby. I know you understand every word I say." But please forgive me if I don't answer. Life is great just the way it is and I'm not going to spoil it.

Selby

ABOUT THE AUTHOR

Duncan Ball is an Australian author and scriptwriter, best known for his popular books for children. Among his most-loved works are the Selby books of stories plus the collections *Selby's Selection, Selby's Joke Book* and *Selby's Side-Splitting Joke Book*. Some of these books have also been published in New Zealand, Germany, Japan and the USA, and have won countless awards, most of which were voted by the children themselves.

Among Duncan's other books are the Emily Eyefinger series about the adventures of a girl who was born with an eye on the end of her finger, and the comedy novels *Piggott Place* and

Piggotts in Peril, about the frustrations of twelve-year-old Bert Piggott forever struggling to get his family of ratbags and dreamers out of the trouble they are constantly getting themselves into.

Duncan lives in Sydney with his wife, Jill, and their cat, Jasper. Jasper often keeps Duncan company while he's writing and has been known to help by walking on the keyboard. Once, returning to his work, Duncan found the following word had mysteriously appeared on screen: lkantawq . . . .

150